A Body Parts and Other Ar

CW00400325

Cadaver One

From The Heart at Stake Archives.

The Stable family – Vampire hunters

A Body Parts

'That's all very well, but why me? Why now? What the hell does it mean Doctor?'

Jason Jamnick fixed Dr Jacqui Feldman with a steely glare that shouted,' I want answers not procrastination.'

'As I have explained before, I cannot answer your questions as fully as I would like to, Dr Jamnick. Your condition is a very unusual one and I have to be scrupulously honest with you. The cardiologist at The John Radcliffe Hospital and his team are unable to offer a diagnosis or prognosis based on their current knowledge of your condition. It is likely that further tests and evaluation will be required. I'm afraid I can't elaborate further.'

Jacqui Feldman disliked uncertainty, but had come to a decision after discussions with the other partners in the practice on how best to handle Jason Jamnick's unique situation. This was not a case where she could make broad generalisations by casting a wide, deep net and hope that at some point what she suggested would be a close approximation to the actual truth.

'So they don't know what the hell is wrong with me. Is that what you're saying?'

'No Dr Jamnick, you are quite right, they do not know or understand what is the matter with you, or what it may mean.'

Jason Jamnick's resigned expression was half way between a smug confirmation that they didn't know, and the knowing that this only prolonged the uncertainty that would lead to a cure.

'You have another appointment with Mr Carruthers in two weeks time I understand?'

'Yes, in eighteen days, for all the good it will do.'

'Has your general demeanour improved at all? How do you feel on a daily basis now?'

Jason sat forward in the chair, resting his elbows on his knees and bringing the finger tips of both hands up to his lips, as though praying to the doctor. A joke flitted into his mind. *What's the difference between God and a doctor? God knows he's not a doctor.* He betrayed no outward indication of humour.

'I suppose I feel about the same as the last time I saw you. Some days are better than others, I would say. Yesterday for instance I felt lethargic, I had no energy and yet my appetite is strong. It's all rather strange.'

'Hmm - strange is the word, Dr Jamnick.'

She made a note on a pad.

'Have you fainted again?'

'Not recently. The pills you gave me seem to have worked, although as I've said, I still get extremely tired. Exhausted really.'

Jacqui Feldman remained silent for a moment, working out where to take this next. She wanted to at least try and relieve some of his anxiety. She realised what she should do immediately but held back, being sure what Dr Jamnick's response would be.

'Dr Jamnick I know we've been through everything with a fine tooth comb but could I ask you to detail everything once more, just in case I've missed something? I know it's an imposition but I need to be sure in my own mind I've got everything.'

Jason eyed her with suspicion, then looked resigned but did not refuse her request.

'I returned home after a year's sabbatical in Egypt about five months ago. I was studying some artefacts there. I had been home for a week or two and returned to my work at Oxford before things began to change.

I fainted for the first time a little under four months ago. I didn't think too much of it at the time. I had been under a lot of stress at work as I had several reports to write up and papers to publish regarding my recent field trips. I thought it was just one of those things. I dislike being ill and taking time off as I love my work. But twenty four hours after collapsing I had a series of wild palpitations, like a panic attack. It was as though surges of adrenalin were shooting through me. It lasted for some minutes and left me feeling completely drained. My heart was banging wildly and it must have affected my blood pressure because I began to experience strange sensations in my head. My heart beat was all over the place and I couldn't catch my breath. It took all my self control not to black out completely again. That was bad enough, but when it happened again four days later, I became scared, very scared. I mean, I'm only thirty four.'

He shifted in the chair and took a long sigh.

Jacqui Feldman made some more notes, pausing as she thought of what to write, before looking up.

'That is totally understandable Dr Jamnick. I remember when you first came to see me you were confused about your symptoms. You couldn't put your finger on what was going on.'

'Confused? That's an understatement. I was disorientated as well, to the point of not knowing or recognising who and where I was. It was unnerving, like being a mindless automaton, if I can put it in those terms.'

'How long did you experience that sense of vacancy?'

Jason thought for a moment.

'Probably no more than a few seconds, although it seemed far, far longer.'

5

Dr Feldman held his gaze for a moment before writing another note.

'I have difficulty in connecting your physiological symptoms, your cardio-vascular and psychological problems.'

'You mean my heart on the one hand and the fainting and panic attacks on the other?'

'Yes, put simply. Between my diagnosis and the subsequent findings from the cardiac unit, all the common problems and causes that your symptoms may indicate have been eliminated. So there is no cardiac arrhythmia in the accepted sense that we understand, nor is there a tachycardia or a bradycardia – I mean a heart rate that is either too fast or too slow.'

'So what diagnosis would you give to a thirty four year old man who appears to have three separate heartbeats?'

Jacqui Feldman looked down at her notes and shook her head.

◉

Jason Jamnick walked lethargically through the path around Christ Church Meadow. He often walked around the Meadow when he had a break at the University to clear his head. It lay to the south of the Oxford University site and at its southern tip the Meadow was bordered by the River Thames on the west side and the River Cherwell to the east.

Six months ago he would have found it rejuvenating, even therapeutic. Now, signed off work for a further three months, he was trying to follow some of the doctor's advice and not degenerate into someone who, faced with a health problem, believes that the only recourse to restoration of health is by resting and doing as little as possible. That way, surely, lay the path towards indolence and sterility. In any case, he couldn't be like that. He had always having been active.

The day was exceedingly warm and, despite his funereal pace he was beginning to perspire. It was a green oasis in a suburban area. A little further on from the Meadow there was a children's playground and some of the people who passed him were young mothers with small children.

He was absorbed in his own thoughts and problems and paid no attention to his surroundings. He was still coming to terms with Dr Feldman's revelation two days earlier, that the faintest of the three heartbeats detected in his chest cavity, the one they had not detected in tests conducted earlier was, in fact, his own. How the hell had they missed that? What did that say about the other two heartbeats that were apparently so much stronger?

He was grateful that he was on tranquillisers. Without them he would crack up.

Weariness was forcing him to rest so, almost absent-mindedly, he stopped and braced himself with his hands against a tree trunk that grew at a junction of paths. He took a long deep breath and then looked around and felt, just for a moment, something akin to enjoyment of being in this moment. Then it passed and he was once more in the dark foreboding world that had become his reality over the past few months.

As he stared vacantly across the Meadow he became aware of some mumbling from a couple of mothers with pushchairs as they ambled past him. As he came back from his reverie he glanced towards them and noticed that even though they had walked past him, they were turning to look at him, talking animatedly. They exchanged a couple of glances and shared some view point then turned away and continued towards the playground.

Jason had never understood the predilection for gossip and an interest in what other people were up to. Still, he acknowledged that if they knew that he had three heart beats, then he would certainly be subject to a lot more gossip, and not of a pleasant kind.

He stood up and began to walk slowly, completely un-refreshed by his short repose. The sun was directly in front of him and, with no sunglasses, he had to shield his eyes from their powerful rays. A young girl pushing a buggy and holding a toddler by some reins drew level with him. A smile flitted across her face then evaporated, her eyes looking straight through him. She stopped abruptly, staring at the path immediately behind him. He too halted, puzzled by her reaction.

'You got some funny shadow there mate. Is that a trick or what?'

Perplexed, Jason followed the line of her eyes, until he too saw what had grabbed her attention. His shadow, instead of being a silhouette of his own body outline was broken into a least five parts and these were all moving, forming and un-forming, shapes that bore no relation to his own outline. He stood transfixed, watching the various parts of his shadow dance and whirl, moving like iron filings on a sheet of paper as if drawn by a magnet underneath.

The girl remained watching, mesmerized it seemed by the performance. After a further twenty seconds or so the parts of his silhouette merged back and reformed into his own contoured shape. Even when it was over, both he and the girl stayed rooted, watching in case it started again. Jason looked at the girl, whose eyes were enquiring, perhaps even a little fearful. He smiled weakly and shrugged his shoulders in an empty gesture, before thinking that he had caught too much sun. He turned and shuffled away, muttering to himself, fearing that he was going mad.

◉

Jason Jamnick groaned and turned over, becoming awake. His head was pounding, his mouth and throat felt like the bottom of a parrot's cage and he needed to relieve himself. Yet even the simple action of pulling back the duvet cover was arduous and exhausting. God he felt bruised and battered all over. He turned his head to the left and the glowing numbers on his clock told him that it was twenty minutes before four. He lay awake staring at the ceiling, with his hands placed behind his head contemplating absolutely nothing.

When he moved it was a snap decision and a monumental effort to get up and go to the toilet. He stumbled a few times, once over a novel, *The Ka of Gifford Hilary* by Dennis Wheatley, but came back, drained the glass of water by the bedside and pulled the duvet back over himself. He lay like this for perhaps two minutes, his mind devoid of any thoughts whatsoever, before some intriguing and troublesome images filtered into his head.

Initially he relived the incidents with his shadow the day before. He searched vainly for some explanation of what he had witnessed but failed. Could it just have been a trick of the light? Was his eyesight failing in some way? But that wouldn't explain the girl who had drawn his attention to the phenomenon. He could find no plausible rationalization.

Then, he began to see himself in bed asleep, as if from on high. What the hell did that mean? Was he having an out-of-the-body-experience? As he contemplated this possibility he became aware that he hadn't been alone in observing his sleeping physical form. So what did that mean and how was he supposed to interpret it? There had been others floating and swirling above his inert physical body, of that he was convinced. His throbbing head had eased a little but as he forced himself to focus and concentrate his resources towards the buried images somewhere in his mind, he could feel it returning with a vengeance. Still he persisted but his level of anxiety rose at the level of focus required. Words, language came to him but nothing he could recognize. Everything was unintelligible gobbledegook.

Then, suddenly, there they were, milling about in an ethereal mosaic, two other human forms. He audibly gasped at the clarity of his perception as he observed these spectral forms within his mind's eye. He could make out that they were both male, but the hazy wraithlike quality of the images made further features difficult to discern. He shut his eyes tightly in frustration and this seemed, miraculously to enhance the aura of both figures. They seemed familiar somehow.

The throbbing in his temples hadn't eased at all and as his focus slipped away, the pain gained a foothold again. 'This is getting tedious' he thought, and he drew back the duvet cover, collected the empty glass and made for the bathroom to refill it. He drained the first full glass before refilling a second and making his way back to bed. Now fully awake he decided that sleep was probably not going to return, certainly not easily. He re-arranged the pillows behind him and then leant down and picked up the novel from the floor. He hadn't read this in years and only started it a few days ago. He began reading.

◉

Jason Jamnick was asleep and yet his body was being thrown around, thrashing from side to side in a series of paroxysms. His eyes remain closed throughout the turmoil, but as his body shook like a rat in a Jack Russell's mouth, other distortions and contortions took place inside him as though he were being repeatedly punched by unknown, unseen fists.

The distensions from within became increasingly violent and protracted, continuing for some minutes before gradually subsiding and eventually ceasing altogether. Whatever was taking place inside him, Jason Jamnick appeared for the moment to be quiescent.

He lay on his pillow, his face covered in sweat and contorted with exertion. Suddenly his eyes flew open and he scoured the room from his prone position before sitting up in bed. Then, almost in slow motion, he raised his two arms and formed a rigid U shape with his arms bent upwards at the elbow. His lips began to move as if uttering some form of incantation, but the voice was soft, light and uttered in a strange tongue. After he had spoken these invocatory mutterings, during which time the figure of Jason Jamnick had remained serene and dignified, his demeanour began to change. The eyes closed once more and his body lowered to a supine position and lay still.

After an hour his peace is brutally interrupted by a repeat of the bodily intrusions, as though there was a battle taking place within him. His whole body was thrown around like a rag doll. There appeared to be no consciousness within his inert form while the violent assaults on his physical body continued. Then slowly, almost methodically, the gross distortions and movements reduced in intensity before evaporating completely, leaving his body outwardly at peace. Such a judgment would however, be misplaced, for a battle of sorts continued to be waged but at a level and experience, unknown and unseen by the majority of mortal men.

Three hours passed before Jason Jamnick awoke, himself again. He felt exhausted, drained, battered and bruised, neither rested nor refreshed after a night's sleep. He lurched between a hazy awareness of consciousness, and brief periods of clarity, punctured by episodes of utter fatigue and paralysis. That said, as he lay there, he became dimly aware, somewhere in his unconscious, of the presence of others. Slowly he built a picture of what had been happening to him over the past few months. It was so unbelievable, bizarre and beyond human reason and understanding.

He leant down and picked up the novel, The Ka of Gifford Hilary from the floor and quickly leafed through the pages. He found the extract he was looking for and read it aloud to himself,

My feelings were extraordinarily mixed. Shock, horror, amazement and dismay jostled one

another in my whirling mind. It was still striving to grasp the idea that it had suddenly

11

become disembodied; yet no other explanation fitted the facts. Although I no longer had

feeling in any part of myself the conscious 'me' was still standing beside the table, while

sprawled on the floor lay my corpse.

He had read that a few days ago and yet it's full impart had not registered at the time. He admonished himself for not realising it sooner but on more thoughtful reflection admitted to himself that he had been aware for some time, but had chosen to repress these thoughts for fear of being overwhelmed, like Gifford Hilary. In any case, who would believe it possible? He remained in this semi-conscious contemplative state until just before dawn, at which point he felt able to get up to relieve himself and have something to eat and drink. At least, he mused, carrying out those tasks was a welcome return to normality. But then he realised he was going to have to consult his research papers and academic database to try to discover if there was anything available that might help prevent what was happening to him. He knew enough to know that he didn't have much time left.

◉

Three encyclopaedic old and worn texts lay open before him on a table. Jason scribbled some hieroglyphs and then some English translations onto a sheet of A4 paper. He had been reading and researching for over six hours without a break. But he was going to have to take one now because he needed a drink and the toilet. He returned to the table and continued from where he had left off.

He had thankfully experienced no more 'episodes' as he had begun to term them. In fact, he had warmed to his task, feeling peculiarly invigorated and energized. But then it occurred to him that maybe with being away from the museum and antiquities he looked after and studied, as well as the bit of teaching he did, his mind was probably grateful for some academic stimulation.

He collated his writings, which amounted to in excess of ten pages of A4, and read through them meticulously, correcting an error here or there, adding a little, deleting others or merely clarifying something by further research. On several occasions he checked the internet and researched something, but also took the opportunity to contact some of his colleagues at the museum. Without being alarmist, had asked them questions in vague terms. He did not want to appear ridiculous or just plain crazy.

As a research fellow attached to the Faculty of Oriental Studies at Oxford University, he had just completed a year's sabbatical, studying some Ancient Egyptian texts dating from approximately 1600 – 1200BCE held at the Cairo Museum. He had gone out to a number of sites that were being excavated around the capital and had only been back at work for a week or two before he began to experience the abnormal heartbeats and subsequent symptoms. He was, in effect hypothesizing that there was a link between the two. The evidence before him was that he had been studying The Book of the Dead and The Coffin Texts. One of the field trips included a burial site chamber that suggested it may have been constructed for some important advisors, for there were two sets of funereal artefacts and stelae. But Jason was unsure how far he wanted to go in trying to demonstrate a link. He had perused a collection of papyrus documents and fragments while in Cairo and he recalled that one in particular had caught his attention and intrigued him because it didn't seem to fit anywhere into the accepted scheme or pattern of what was currently known and accepted of Ancient Egyptian funeral rites and practices. He had unearthed a copy of some of these ancient manuscripts and a further scrap of papyrus, all that remained of a far larger piece that had also captured his imagination.

On enquiring further the other archaeologists and staff had agreed that both of these documents were unusual and it had been at that moment that they had shown him a rather ugly figurine that, it was suggested featured in certain types of funeral ceremony. The scrap of papyrus and the figurine were linked, although it was unclear exactly how, but his hosts at one of the excavation sites had suggested that they were part of a divine rite of reincarnation. This aspect, though, had never been taken seriously by academia and so was largely ignored. That was until Jason began to make a closer academic investigation. The papyrus fragment still contained significant instructions and beatifications for Jason to decipher, but he had made steady progress, up until when he had started to feel ill.

He prepared a glass of water on the table and placed the figurine to one side. The Cairo Museum had been persuaded to lend it to the university for Jason to study, and now he began to recite what was inscribed on the papyrus fragment, reading from his English translation.

He read;

'May Isis kneel over you and wash your newborn form, may she set you on the good path of those who are judged innocent in the face of any enemies who'd accuse you before the judges of Tomb-world on the blessed day you pass beyond.'

Jason paused reflectively, waiting for something to happen. When, after a few moments, nothing had changed, he traced back to where he had got to and continued with his recital;

'Homage to you great God, the Lord of the double Ma'at, I have come to you my Lord I have brought myself here to behold your beauties, I know you and I know your name.'

He had no idea whether what he was saying and doing would have any effect, but he didn't feel he had a choice. He had to do something, now that he was sure what was happening. Without further ado, he continued with the negative confessions, declaring himself innocent of any wrongdoing against the gods or his fellow man,

'I am pure, I am pure, I am pure, I am pure.'

On the fourth repeat of the negative confession declaration, Jason's eyes began to move from side to side. Something, although he wasn't sure what, was happening. Slowly, like a crawling mist enveloping him, he felt his own self, his own thoughts and personality in his own mind being pushed to one side and replaced...no, he thought, not replaced but somehow lying alongside his own. So although still aware and conscious of himself, there was something or, more accurately, someone else in his head, whom it appeared had some control over his body as well as his mind.

Without conscious will or thought his mouth began to move involuntarily. Quietly his mouth uttered the words and slowly, as though emerging through a thick, almost impenetrable fog he realised that the words he was saying originated from the full negative confessions from the Papyrus of Ani. This was from the complete Declaration of Innocence from the Book of the Dead that dated from 1240 BCE. As soon as he had recited the full set of declarations which totalled over forty in number he began to recite from the Papyrus of Nu, also from the Book of the Dead. He ended this slightly shorter avowal with a repeat of the series of negative confessions with which he had started;

'I am pure, I am pure, I am pure. My pure offerings are the pure offerings of that great Benu which dwelleth in Hensu. For behold I am the nose of Neb-nefu, the lord of the air who giveth sustenance unto all mankind on the day of the filling of the Utchat in Anu, in the second month of the season, Pert on the last of the month in the presence of the Lord of this earth. I have seen the filling of the Utchat in Anu, therefore let not calamity befall me in this land or in the Hall of Maati because I know the names of the gods who are therein and who are the followers of the Great God.'

Jason's mouth stopped reciting and for a moment he thought that was it, but with no conscious instruction or thought his right hand moved towards the left side of his body and hovered just above his heart, before lowering and covering it. Again his mouth started moving, without him wishing it to.

'Pay good heed to the weighing in the Balance of the heart of the Osiris, the singing woman of Amen. Anhai whose word is truth and place thou her heart in the seat of truth in the presence of the Great God.'

It took Jason some moments to realise that this recitation came from the weighing of the heart ceremony which was part of the speech given by the dweller in the embalmment chamber as Anubis, master of ceremonies, led the deceased by the hand to the scales in the Hall of Maat. While he was aware of being part of his own consciousness he didn't feel particularly concerned at what was taking place. But now he felt the other 'consciousness' within his head begin to fade away, only to be gradually replaced by a consciousness that seemed altogether more substantial and consuming.

'Ahhh,' he screamed as the pain and pressure began to increase as some strange kind of battle for possession was waged in his head. He was sure that there were no specific rituals, chants, incantations or spells that would prevent what was happening to him, but rather than do nothing, he decided that reciting some of the accepted declarations and judgment spells and incantations might register some effect. These would have been performed at funereal ceremonies of mummification through embalmment to protect the deceased in readiness for the corpse's passage through the underworld and its resurrection in the afterlife. Not exactly akin to his own situation, he knew, but some of the texts were used to placate the gods and demonstrate the inherent goodness and righteous moral conduct shown by the deceased when they were alive. Maybe, he reasoned, if he highlighted his own case sufficiently, that might slow down or even prevent what was happening to him.

His head felt as if it might explode. Just then, he realised what was going on. This new consciousness wasn't replacing the previous one, it was trying to somehow lie alongside the initial one and his own. There were three different consciousnesses vying for space within his psyche. Despite the throbbing that permeated his skull, he saw glimpses of memory from the other two, giving his own mind's eye a sighting of the identities of his two usurpers.

There was a large audience hall with a man, clearly a Pharaoh, seated on a richly inlaid throne atop a large dais, keenly paying attention to a gaggle of men below him.

Within the hall were many men, although they appeared to be split into two groups, one of two and another of seven or eight. Two appeared to be of greater importance than the others and seemed to be arguing with the others. A rod was thrown on the floor at the feet of the pharaoh and immediately it turned into a serpent. The larger group of men began to laugh, clearly taunting the pair as each one cast a rod at the feet of the Pharaoh each rod metamorphosing into a serpent. The original snake reared up and grew to giant size, consuming the eight smaller ones, much to the chagrin of the larger group of men.

Jason saw all this as clearly as if it were happening right in front of him. The throbbing in his head had calmed as he lived through the vision, but now as his concentration wavered it returned with a vengeance.

'Ahhhgggg,' he screamed once more as the load within his skull threatened to implode. The burden within his head disappeared, leaving him with heightened perception became heightened. He heard whispers, increasing in volume.

'Jannes and Jambres,' he shouted out loud, finally identifying and naming his assailants.

In his head he heard them answer.

'Yes.'

'You are the two Egyptian magicians who contested with Aaron and Moses.'

'We will respond in your tongue even though you have some limited knowledge of ours. We are not to be taken lightly. We require a vessel and you have been chosen.'

'What will happen to me?'

The sorcerers considered their response.

'You will cease to exert any meaningful control over this receptacle.'

'So I will die?'

'You will. A mortal death.'

'And you expect me to relinquish control of my body, without putting up a fight?'

'Any form of resistance is futile. Over three thousand years ago we embarked on a journey to the heavens after gaining the necessary occult knowledge. We were not welcomed but we gained access to the first heavens and the angels could not evict us because of the potent talismans that adorn our finery. You have nothing that approaches our experience. You are merely a mortal creature.'

'A mortal creature I may be, but you are missing one essential detail.'

'And what would that be?'

'You were defeated and thrown out of heaven without even being aware of it.'

Silence reigned in Jason's head as the two conjurors digested his analysis.

'You lie!'

'If that were the case you would be in the seventh heaven now and not trying to steal my body. You were tricked and the trick is you don't even know it.'

'Even Michael or Gabriel themselves could not defeat us. Only they could remove us from the heavens.'

'That much has substance, but defeated you were, as your presence here now shows.'

Jason could hear their whispered discussions, too faint for him to make out what they were saying.

'Tell us what you think you know, mortal.'

Jason laughed out loud.

'And reveal the only advantage I have? What strategy of strength is that?'

Jason had recalled from more recent research that Jannes and Jambres had managed to ascend to the 5th heaven but there had met an angel who was accommodating and considered, and had shown not the slightest indication of anger or defiance. The two magicians had been lured into a false sense of security based in large part on their own narcissism and infallibility. They had removed their talismans, which made them extremely vulnerable. Thus exposed, the two sorcerers were thrown out of the 5th heaven with a mere wave of the angel's hand which also had the advantageous corollary of clearing any memory of the event from their minds.

'There is an alternative.'

Jason felt the pressure against the plates of his skull as the two magicians tried to torture the information out of him. He laughed once more.

'You haven't learnt much over those three thousand years have you?'

'You underestimate us, mortal.'

'No, but you underestimate me,' Jason grimaced as the pain spread across his temples and enveloped his cranium.

'Do you recall the plagues of blood, frogs and gnats that resulted from your Pharaoh's stubbornness?' Jason's face was contorted with pain but he managed to force out the words between his gritted teeth.

For Jason the silence that followed spoke volumes about the doubts he was planting within the two magicians. He summoned up all his strength to utter his decisive recitation; the one he knew could banish the two sorcerers from his head.

'*Damnatio memoriae.*' Immediately he felt a relaxation in the pressure in his skull.

'*Damnatio memoriae,*' he repeated, then said the chant again and again, each time feeling the two presences in his head dissipate until eventually he could detect neither of them at all. He felt better physiologically; his heart beat returned to normal.

Jason's final incantation was from the Apocrypha and banished the names of the two magicians by denying their existence and therefore their bodily accretion and physical form.

Jason slumped back in his chair, mentally and physically exhausted. And yet he still couldn't let it go.

He sat contemplating his experience and reasoned that it was probably for the best if he kept all this to himself. He looked down at his hands and found that they were holding the figurine, the *ushabti*. He reasoned that this particular *ushabti* was probably used in a magical ceremony when one of the sorcerers had died and he had had his Ka transferred into the figurine so it functioned as his alter ego. Then when he had begun handling and examining it, the essence of the sorcerer had permeated into his physical body. That would explain why the presence of one of the magicians was so powerful and dominant compared to the other.

◉

'Well I'm pleased to tell you Dr Jamnick that I can give you a clean bill of health. Everything is now back the way it should be. How do you feel in yourself?'

Jason smiled at Jacqui Feldman. It was true he was fine, more than fine. Since he had purged himself of the two sorcerers a week ago, he had grown stronger and stronger, better in every way than before. It was almost as though they had provided some boost to his body. Like much of what had happened, he would keep it to himself though.

'Very good, Doctor. I returned to work two days ago and have completed my reports and begun writing a paper. Could it have been a virus or some bug I picked up in Egypt?'

Dr Feldman cast her eyes over the notes in front of her.

'I suppose it could. There doesn't appear to be any other explanation. I don't like to admit failure Dr Jamnick but I really am at a loss here, it is bizarre. But then none of us are magicians are we?'

He smiled and let out an audible sigh. He had decided he would explain it away by having picked up a virus of some sort while he had been away. That would serve as a cover story and was plausible without being able to be dismissed or checked as to its authenticity.

He knew now, that he had been engaged in a battle for possession with the two magicians. The Egyptians believed the individual to be composed of five parts; The Ren, or an individual's name; the Ib, the heart, the seat of your soul; the Sheut, or shadow; the Ba, that which makes each of us unique and different and finally the Ka, the vital essence, the difference between the living and the dead. They had tried to take possession of him on all those fronts, but mercifully, had failed.

'I suppose not. I am just relieved that I now have only one heart beat. I don't miss the other two at all.

The End

The Crawling Skin

God she thought to herself, this was soooooooooooo boring! Having to smile and be pleasant to relatives you didn't know existed and would probably never see again was bad enough. But then some of them actually wanted to *talk* to you. But talk to you not because they were concerned or remotely interested in YOU as a person. Oh no, it wasn't that they cared about you; they just wanted to extract as much information from you as they possibly could.

Eliane Delves sat on a low wall at the rear of the church. Yes, they would squeeze as much out of you as they could, so that they could then bathe themselves in the raw, warm sunshine of that knowledge, convinced that they knew you and everything about you. Then, secure in that knowledge, they owned a piece of you, a piece of you was theirs.

The bells were commemorating the marriage between cousin Sebastien and....now what was her stupid, ridiculous name....Cassandra, yes that was it, Cassandra; and if Eliane was told by one more relative that everyone and anyone was to call her Cassie because that was what she wanted, she would scream.

The service had ended twenty minutes earlier. The majority of the congregation had followed the newly married couple and Angus, the photographer, to a secluded part of the church gardens. As Angus tried to organise the wedding party, Eliane thought she might throw up if she didn't steal herself away. While her parents' attention was diverted by Angus' activities, she walked coldly away towards the back of the church where she could be undisturbed and free. She had sat on the wall and got her mobile out to check to see if she had missed any calls or messages. She hadn't, not that she was expecting any, so she had played a few games on it before she got bored with that, then she began to think about why she was there in the first place. After a moment of concentrated thought she came to the conclusion that she didn't know, but could lay the blame fully at her parents' door....again.

Eliane showed no interest in the architecture of the 14th century church, nor in the myriad of gravestones that littered the church grounds on three sides. Closer inspection would have revealed to her that some dated from the eighteenth century and some featured very young people who had died well before their time. But you don't consider death or not being around when you're twelve years old. In fact there is only a very narrow band of subject matter of interest to a twelve year old girl. Except that Eliane Delves was not your everyday sort of twelve year old girl, not by a long way.

Finally deciding that she'd had enough of sitting alone, Eliane jumped down from the wall and slowly, resignedly, made her way around to the front of the church. The grounds were completely devoid of people. That was what she thought at first, anyway. Then, as she passed the main church door, she recalled that the site allocated for the photographs was a small hidden arbour further up to her left and behind the church, so she continued along the path. But as she did so she scratched her forehead. She stopped just past the still open church door where she began to experience a strange tingling sensation. It was a prickly feeling, which started at the top of her head and gradually washed down through her body from her shoulders, arms, trunk and finally to her legs before petering out as though it had passed through her feet and into the ground.

Well, that was very strange, she thought to herself and began walking again. But before she had taken two strides, the tremors, which were like millions of tiny insects crawling across her skin, began their journey from her head down to her toes once again, more marked this time, almost painful. She stopped abruptly and looked down the length of her body, intrigued by the sensation. She was not a twelve year old who spooked easily. It had happened before but then she had felt only curiosity, not fear. There would be a straightforward explanation.

She continued her promenade towards the arbour. As she turned the first corner where the chancel and vestry joined the nave, a slight movement out of the corner of her right eye stopped her in her tracks. At the very moment she stopped, a great wave of the tingling sensation erupted through her whole body. It made her dizzy, and as she turned slightly to her right she came face to face with a young boy slouched up against the church, eyeing her suspiciously. She thought he was young because of his size, but as she met him eye to eye she realised that there was something about his look that made him seem far more mature. The tingling sensation was like an alarm going off, but there was no one to turn it off. The boy glared at her, a slightly hostile expression on his face, but he said nothing.

Eliane stood transfixed at first, then tore her eyes away from his and carried on walking along the path to the arbour. She turned once to look back and saw him staring after her, although he hadn't moved at all.

It was only when she rejoined the rest of the congregation, all milling around the bride and groom, Angus now having finished, that she realised the crawling sensation had diminished in intensity the further away from the boy she walked. Now it had disappeared completely. THAT was very strange. Who was the boy and why did he provoke that reaction in her?

•

Three days after the wedding, when she had thought it through by herself, Eliane asked her mother at home about the possible identity of the boy.

'I'd say he was younger than me, about eight or nine maybe. But his expression and the way he....acted, he seemed a lot older, somehow'

Eliane's mother looked at her daughter. She longed for her to make a connection with another human being and become a little more grown up ; although that wasn't really a fair assessment, she realised. Eliane was a strange child, too grown up in some ways, always having problems with authority and with being told what to do. Still, for Eliane to show an interest in another human being was not an everyday occurrence, so she had better make the most of it. It might not happen again for a long time.

'I think you mean Emery. He's a cousin on Father's side. He's an only child too, like you.'

Eliane glanced at her mother but remained silent.

'Although your father doesn't talk to his brother Bernard much, but Aunt Valerie and I have the occasional long rant on the telephone. We had a couple of little chats at the wedding and she did say that she and Uncle Bernard were worried about Emery.'

'Why?'

'Well, you're not to go telling all and sundry now Eli, are you?'

'Mother, I'm not a child!'

'Hmmm yes I know. Emery's being difficult with other people. He just doesn't like them.'

'You mean he's becoming misanthropic?' She spoke the word slowly and distinctly, as if reading it from a page.'You can use long words with me, mother, I do understand.'

'Yes, yes Eli, sorry, it's an old habit. Valerie says he seems almost to hate and despise people, absolutely detests them. She said he had shouted something like, 'everyone's evil and they're all so selfish and inward looking,' in temper at her when she tried to question him about it. It's making his school life difficult. I mean, it's one thing to not get on with other children. But to be constantly at odds, aggressive and confrontational with his teachers is causing something of a major issue. Valerie said that he'll end up getting expelled if he doesn't modify his behaviour.'

Eliane looked at her mother crossly.

'Has anyone asked HIM why he thinks he acts the way he does? Has anyone asked HIM why he hates and despises people?' God, she could identify with that.

'Of course they have. He went to a child psychologist a few years ago. I don't think it was very successful, as Emery accused the psychologist of all sorts of unpleasant things, so Valerie said at the time, so I don't suppose they'll want to repeat that for some time yet.'

'Maybe he just needs a friend? You know, someone who he feels he can talk to, confide in maybe about the way he feels.'

Her mother looked at Eliane with a slightly amused expression on her face.

'What?'

'The phrase pot and kettle comes to mind, Eli Delves. When was the last time you confided in a friend?'

Eliane looked at her mother blankly.

'I don't have any friends.'

'Exactly. You know, now I come to think of it, you and Emery are alike. You have the same outlook on life.'

'From what you've said he doesn't seem normal at all.'

'It depends on your definition of normal doesn't it? I mean – what's normal?'

Eliane made a noise somewhere between a grunt and a hrrmph.

'I don't want to be normal, it's boring. I want to be different.'

'I know, and you are. We all are, it's just that some people have to show everyone else that they are different rather than just accepting it and embracing their differences within themselves.'

'What, like Leah Congdon's mother shaving all her hair off?'

'Well, yes sort of.'

'So normal can be whatever you want it to be?'

'We are who and what we are, we are all normal. It's just that those at the margins, on the periphery of society, are questioned sometimes, a lot of the time, they are not accepted by those in the middle.'

'The boring ones you mean?'

'I mean the ones who perhaps through no fault of their own have a strong tendency to conform, a reluctance to question the status quo. You know what that means, Eli, don't you?'

'So you mean those who just accept everything without asking why, who, how or where?'

'Yes, in a way.'

Eliane pondered this for a moment, her expression softening.

'So what you're saying is Emery is normal, even for a boy of ten?'

•

'Do I have to go?'

'Eliane Delves, you may think you are twelve years old going on twenty three but there is no way you are staying at home on your own while your mother and I attend Uncle Egbert's funeral. Do I make myself clear? Now - discussion over. Go and get ready.'

With a single, sullen nod of her head Eliane did what her father said and went upstairs to change, without further protest. In actual fact she wasn't as unwilling to attend the funeral as she had made out for the past hour and a half, but she thought she may as well try. In any case, she reasoned, it would be what her parents expected her to do. It wasn't the funeral of a particularly close relative, just some distant male relation of her father's. What had caught her interest about all this was his name, or at least the name that he was referred to by the family, I mean, she thought, who was called Egbert these days? That might have been enough on its own to have triggered her curiosity and willingness to attend, but the prospect of encountering the strange Emery once again was, she admitted to herself, the primary reason for making as little fuss over going as she had.

Eliane began rifling through her wardrobe and drawers trying to pick out something suitable, yet would still make a statement about her.

Her bedroom was bare; bereft of posters on the wall, no soft toys on her bed and a plain, empty, white colour scheme. Some would have said sterile.

There was little in the way of make-up, perfume or girl's toiletries of any description. In fact her only inclusions, save for the furniture of a bed and bedside table, wardrobe, chest of drawers and a desk was a large, overflowing bookcase and a laptop. A pile of CDs were stacked on the desk, although nowadays she downloaded any music she wanted.

She did enjoy clothes, although they tended to be a conservative black or shades of grey, but had some white clothing and that is what she would have chosen had she been allowed. But she wasn't permitted that freedom so resorted to the colour of darkness.

Despite her predominantly dark clothing she had no gothic influences, save a few bands here and there. She didn't feel the need to identify and align herself with any sort of group or movement.

She had almost finished changing when her father bellowed up the stairs, reminding her that she had to wear all dark clothing, black if possible, although dark blue would be acceptable. She grimaced in the mirror, annoyed at her father's needless intervention and now resented being told to wear dark clothing. She didn't care one way or the other what she wore, although the occasional bit of variety was welcome, as long as it was her choice. The last time she had attended a funeral she had been allowed to wear other colours and the service had been more a celebration of the person's life. I mean, she thought, he was ninety seven when he died so he'd had something to celebrate, hadn't he?

She put on a pair of black leggings, with a black skirt over the top. She knew she had a plain dark grey T shirt somewhere, but took a moment to find it buried at the bottom of a drawer. She quietly muttered to herself, berating her parents for their perceived annoyances and injustices. She forgot her own willing compliance in going along with them, albeit for her own ends.

The wedding had been a little over two weeks ago, and as she took a final glance at herself in her full length mirror she thought, isn't it always the same with families – you manage to avoid them and keep them at bay for years, no contact at all, and then *bang*, like London buses fate brings them all along together.

She had her own agenda for the funeral, but in case things got boring, she grabbed her mobile phone and checked it was charged. Then she strolled down the stairs, checking her playlists, while her frustrated parents waited.

●

Eliane was miffed. They had driven for over two hours to the church, but had still arrived late. The service was already underway and they were ushered to the back, with only just enough room to squeeze everyone in. Once they had settled, Eliane scoured the congregation in front of her as best she could but couldn't see whether Emery was present or not. Maybe he hadn't come. She'd asked her mother who believed he would be there – if HE wanted to go. So it was up to him, then. She'd have to try that.

At the end of the service they mingled with the other relatives before people left for the wake, but still she couldn't spot Emery. She was seriously starting to wonder whether he had come.

After the funeral most of the family went back to Uncle Charles' for the wake. Charles was the oldest of Egbert's children, being in his seventies. His cottage was in a leafy glade, smothered in ivy and honeysuckle.

As Eliane's father drew up outside one of the other children was acted as parking attendant, guiding the vehicles towards a parking spot.

'It's filling up quickly,' said Eliane's mother as another three cars pulled up behind them, waiting to be directed.

The sun was shining and Eliane was desperate to catch a glimpse of Emery, just to confirm that he was there.

The cottage was a large sprawling affair with several nooks and crannies on the ground floor in addition to those larger rooms you would expect to be present. Eliane left her parent's side the minute she entered the cottage and she took herself off to explore the whole of the ground floor, not only to see if Emery had already arrived, but also to get a feel for the layout of the place. As she went from room to room it was clear that more people were arriving by the minute as the floor space began to disappear. She did so like to know her surroundings, just in case.

After a time she was having to squeeze between the mass of adults mingling about in the various rooms. There were a few young children, all under seven or eight who she chose to ignore, despite one or two of them trying to get her to play with them. One was a particularly persistent little angel of about six, who appeared unmoved by Eliane's cold, stern face that shouted Go Away! Eli resorted to moving through a series of rooms at speed before ducking out into the garden, leaving them all behind. She considered why it was that children failed to read body language and facial expressions. She decided that they probably hadn't yet developed the means to.

Just as she was enjoying her freedom her skin began to tingle and dance. She froze, knowing what this meant, but still unable to see Emery physically. Then, without warning, the sensation went off the chart and she felt the most powerful tremors she had so far experienced, pass through her.

She advanced forward a couple of steps on the patio and there, just around a corner stood Emery Dalton watching her intently as she emerged. As their eyes met she felt palpitations flow through her. She thought she might faint but then Emery was standing right by her side, his eyes fixed on her face. How she knew this she wasn't sure, but it did make her feel a little uneasy. This was not a type of feeling she was used to. Although she was significantly taller than Emery, he seemed to dominate her. The tingling sensation had receded but she still felt unnerved.

'You must be Eliane. I asked my mother.' Emery's voice was reedy and high-pitched.

Eliane regarded Emery quizzically as though coming to terms with his presence.

'You must be Emery. I asked *my* mother.'

Now it was Emery's turn to observe Eliane as if he was trying to work out exactly what she had meant by repeating his words. He looked around, suddenly aware of the close proximity of so many other people, the majority of them adults, spilling out from the cottage.

'Come into the garden, there's too many people in here.'

Emery turned. Without glancing back to check that she was following, he forced his way between the ocean of relations, and was gone. Eliane stood rooted to the spot, trying to regain a level of composure and a sense of reality now that the tingling had subsided and she was being ordered around by a child younger than her. But after shrugging her shoulders she followed the direction that Emery had taken, only to be immediately confronted by him and a sinister looking woman.

'Mother, this is her, Eliane. The one I was telling you about.'

Emery's mother looked at Eliane, her mouth open in stupefaction.

'You really talked to this girl, Emery?'

'I did and voluntarily.'

Emery's mother looked from him to Eliane and back again as if trying to comprehend what is was about her that had enabled her son to want to talk to her.

34

'But why this one?'

Emery looked up at his mother without humour or irony, his face a blank.

'She's different.'

His mother opened her mouth to speak but changed her mind and instead addressed Eliane.

'He doesn't talk to anyone, normally.'

'I know. Shall we go?'

And with that dismissive comment Eliane tripped off into the garden, Emery hot on her heels. The crawling skin had returned, although less intense than before.

The garden was large and Eliane waded across an expansive lawn before bearing off to the right where a set of two swings was placed. She sat on one of them glancing at the figure of Emery who was dogging her footsteps at a far slower pace. When he arrived at the swings he ignored the one available but stood, slouching against one of the supporting metal poles.

'Why don't you talk to people?'

'Don't like them,' Emery replied.

'No, neither do I.'

'I know.'

'How do you know?'

'I can tell.'

'You can't know what I'm thinking.'

Emery remained silent as though he were contemplating his response to Eliane's statement.

'You've had a funny tingling feeling like loads of ants crawling all over you, haven't you?'

Eliane looked at him, the truth written on her face.

'Thought so, do you wanna know what it means?'

Eliane opened her mouth to speak but Emery didn't give her the chance.

'But I need to warn you, you won't like it.'

Eliane appeared resigned rather than elated.

'I felt it first at the wedding as I walked past you outside the church.'

'Hmmm maybe then first, it might be different for you and me. I was five when I first noticed it, but I was too young to really understand what was happening.'

'Why does it happen, what's it mean?'

'For me it was the first week of school. I hadn't ever gone to nursery or pre-school or anything like that. I think my parents were worried about my lack of friends, even then. Probably right to. I was fine in the playground with lots of space around, but when we all filed into the assembly hall and sat down I began to feel this funny tickle which spread all over me and wouldn't stop. I didn't know why or what it was. I wasn't worried though. I never worry really, it was just my morbid curiosity wanting to know what it was all about.'

'That sounds like me too. I like to know things. I don't mean about people, boring everyday people. I want to know the how and why of things working in the whole world.'

'Do you read a lot? Not only books but on the internet as well?

'Oh yeah all the time. It drives my parents crazy because I never want to go out.'

Eliane looked at Emery from under her eyebrows and gave a hint of a smile.

'Any friends?'

'Not really. Everyone thinks I'm a little weird, but I don't care. I'm different.'

Now Emery smiled, although it resembled more of a grimace.

'Hmmm yeah, I know that feeling.'

They both looked at each other with a renewed level of respect for the other.

'You're smart too, aren't you?'

Emery seemed pleased with his powers of deduction.

'If you say so.'

'Yeah, so during that first time I sort of had that tingling it was this boy who was sat just behind and a little to one side of me. It took me the whole week to work out it was him that set me off.'

'So why, what's it mean?'

Emery looked at Eliane with a new found seriousness.

'I think it's a sort of 'sense''.

'What, like sight or smell?'

'Sort of, I'm still not completely sure.'

'But a sense for what? I mean it's got to be *for* something, it's got to find something, to give you information. With eyes you can see things, ears you can hear sound, taste you can....taste. So what does this sense do, what does it find out?'

A new expression came onto Emery's face, sheepish and strange. She hadn't seen him like this before.

'Bad things.'

●

Eliane gazed vacantly out of the car window at the hedgerows and blue sky flowing past. She wasn't exactly troubled, but there was a sense within her that after today, nothing, including her, would ever be the same again.

They had left the wake almost half an hour ago. It had been obvious from her demeanour that any attempt on the part of her parents at trying to engage her in conversation, would be met with a stony, albeit contemplative silence. So they hadn't bothered.

She thought about the rest of their conversation. Emery, in spite of his 'I'm still not completely sure' insistence had nevertheless provided a pretty full picture of what he thought was going on, at least from a precocious ten year old's perspective. Only Eliane realised fairly quickly that he possessed similar attributes to her own, one of them being that he was academically ahead compared to his peers. She knew only too well from her own experience and reading that adults found it difficult to deal with such precociousness. They seemed to take it as a threat to their own dominance. For some reason the line, 'no one likes a smart kid' seeped into her head. What it really meant was, 'no grown up likes a smart kid because it makes them feel inadequate and doubt their own intelligence and therefore superiority as well.'

Both of them, it transpired, had played up just to get their parents' attention when they were very young and then, in the blink of an eye, play up even more so they would leave them alone. Of course, it rarely worked out exactly right as adults compute things in an entirely different way, but both of them had that tendency.

They both had an interest in animals and preferred their company probably as a windbreak against unwanted and uncomfortable relationships with human beings. Emery was quite rational and candid with it all, which in turn made it easier for Eliane to be honest with herself.

They had asked each other what was the one thing they would like to do right now. Eliane had had no doubt and recalled a story she had read, about a thirteen year old girl in Mongolia who hunted foxes and hares with a trained Golden Eagle. 'I could do that,' she told Emery, 'in the vast steppes of that wilderness, all that space and few people.'

Emery actually smiled and said he could understand that, although he wasn't sure about the killing of other animals. That had led on to a discussion about predators and prey, and eventually Emery conceded that providing the prey was fully consumed, that was nature red in tooth and claw so was probably acceptable. He thought he might become vegan within a year.

They had returned again to describing the sense and at first Emery had been evasive, especially in terms of the two of them.

'It's not nice, it's not good and you won't like me. I don't want to upset you.'

Eliane was surprised at his reaction, but even more amazed at her own response.

'You won't upset me, Emery. We're too much the same, you and me. We have a connection, things in common. I know you won't upset me, trust me.'

Emery moved away from the swing pole and walked around, kicking at imaginary stones, before coming to a halt in front of Eliane who remained seated on the swing.

'The first time you had that tingling was when you walked past me, without seeing me first, at the church, yeah?'

'Yes.'

'And whenever I've been near you since then?'

'Yes, although it has got a little less tingly, as the distance between us gets bigger.'

'Hmm, well as I said I think it's a...it's a sense that 'sees' bad in people.'

'What, bad like evil you mean?'

'Yes. That's a good word, evil.'

'Oh, that's not good.'

'I did tell you didn't I?'

Eliane looked at Emery a little more warily.

'So...what does this mean really, Emery?'

Emery looked disappointed, as though he were about to let Eliane down.

'Are you sure you want to know?'

•

'But it's already ten past one, when are they going to get here?'

Emery's parents glanced from one to the other and then at their increasingly troublesome, precocious son.

'They are only ten minutes late. Have a little more patience Emery, dear.'

Emery began to pace backwards and forwards, although neither of his parents wanted to remind him AGAIN that he'd wear a hole in the carpet if he kept that up.

After some three minutes a car could be heard pulling up outside the house and Emery was immediately at the window, looking through the net curtain observing the arrivals. Because of the trees and bushes lining the garden path it was difficult for him to be certain who had arrived. He could clearly see the top of Eliane's dad's head but not her mother nor her. He began to get butterflies in the pit of his stomach. The front door was tapped a couple of times and Emery rushed to open it ahead of his mother.

'EMERY!'

Ignoring the castigation he reached up to the door knob, grasping the edge of the door so he could open it more quickly. On the doorstep stood the beaming, but for him so unwelcome, faces of Eliane's parents.....but no Eliane. Emery's face fell and the butterflies in his stomach turned into bats.

'Hello, sorry we're late. As you can see we're one short. Long story, tell you during lunch. I hope you haven't gone to too much trouble on our account.'

Emery stood motionless, rooted to the spot beside the front door, trying to frantically hide his disappointment, but failing majestically.

'What's the matter with Eliane?' he asked, as plaintively as Emery ever got.

'She's not feeling too good I'm afraid. We tried to persuade her....but to no avail. Oh I almost forgot, she asked me to give you this.'

Eliane's mother fished into her handbag and drew out a small envelope and handed it to Emery. He almost snatched it from her and ran for the stairs.

'Manners Emery! Lunch will be in five.'

'Not hungry, don't want any.'

The bedroom door slammed shut, reverberating through the whole house.

'Boys!' said Emery's mother.

'Girls!' said Eliane's father.

Emery slumped on his bed and ripped the envelope open with mounting trepidation. Inside was a single torn scrap of plain white paper. He turned it around to the correct orientation, the bats in his stomach now becoming dragons, and fire breathing dragons at that. He quickly cast his eye over Eliane's short message which was in text speak. It ran;

U no u will c me again BEG

Emery dropped his hands to his lap and sat motionless. He had been so sure she would come! What did he know! So smart and know it all and he couldn't even get this right! He lay back on his bed, his head nestling in the pillows. Had he been wrong to tell her so much? Should he have kept his mouth shut? He began to berate himself further. He was normally an expert at keeping quiet, of keeping things to himself and not giving them away. But then he lightened a little as he realised there had been no choice. There WAS a link, a connection between him and this girl and there was nothing he could have done to prevent it, was there? It had been and was inevitable.

'Are you sure you want to know?'

'Why wouldn't I? It's not like you can see into the future, is it?'

Emery remembered looking at Eliane at that moment on the swing, her wide innocent eyes just betraying something....well something a little more sinister, an acknowledgement as if she'd known something about this all along. He should have realised that she wouldn't have come today. Stupid! It was a game to her now, like Hitman, Grand Theft Auto or Halo, but who was the target and who the assassin? And so he had told her.....everything. He had begun by telling her that the tingling sensation acted like an evil sense triggered by the close proximity of a bad or potentially bad person.

'So because I've had this sensation around you, you are or will become an evil person. Is that what you're saying?'

'Err, no, it's apparently a two way process. I get all creepy skin with you. What you feel is a bounce back type of effect, an echo or a reflection of me sensing you.'

'So eerrmm....I'm the evil one, the potential evil one, is that right?'

'Yeah, that's it.'

Eliane had pondered this for a few moments, her eyes narrowing as she evaluated his revelation, while at the same time she began slowly to build up momentum on the swing, backwards and forwards, backwards and forwards, getting higher and higher.

'So what will I do, can you tell?'

'Oh yeah I can tell. This has been part of me since I was five years old and it develops every year. It's really quiet horrible at times. Right from the start, I could detect even very low levels of bad in people and although kids haven't been exposed to evil, I can still detect

43

its potential in them. So I was getting all tingly and going off here there and everywhere for the first year and a half. Then I began to be able to bring it under some level of control, but that's only really been happening regularly for the past year or so.'

'So are you some good white angel or something then?'

Emery smiled at the recollection of that line.

'Definitely not. You've seen how I am, how I behave around people. I really don't like people because as adults they only really care about themselves. Oh, they may care for family and children and all that, but in their dealings with other adults most are not very pleasant. I remember one history lesson about the French during the war and the teacher said something about 'to do evil all one has to do is not do good or do nothing in the face of evil.' That, as you might understand, struck me somewhat. I don't know where this feeling has come from or what I should or can do with it but it's a part of me and there's nothing I can do about it.'

'So what am I going to do then Emery?'

'Do you really want to know?'

Eliane was now swinging in such a wide high arc that Emery had to take a step or three back away from her.

'Oh yeah.'

'Okay then. Don't blame me, will you?'

Eliane glared down from on high but didn't reply.

'You will kill your parents.'

Eliane continued without pause.

'Can you tell when?'

'Hmm - I'm not exactly sure but in a few years time, maybe five, six.'

Eliane continued higher and higher as the effort she put in increased a little more, although her tone and voice remained calm and neutral.

'But you were aware of that anyway weren't you?'

'Now that you've confirmed it for me, yes I suppose I was.'

Eliane let the swing die down and then, still at a high arc, she leapt off the seat and landed on her feet right next to Emery who involuntarily took a couple of steps backwards.

'And what will *you* do Emery?'

'Do? What will *I* do? I don't know.'

'Well as you said, evil can be doing nothing when faced with evil, can't it? And now that you know what I might be going to do....surely it falls to you to....make sure I don't. No one else knows only you and me....Emery.'

Eliane took two paces towards him and before Emery could react in any way, she reached out with her hand and lightly touched him on the shoulder. He flinched and staggered back a step or two, before falling to the ground on his bottom, clearly in some pain. Eliane smiled with satisfaction.

Then she turned brusquely and walked back to the cottage, pausing briefly to turn around and give Emery a further broad, devilish grin.

'Remember my smile Emery. I'm part of you. I know you can see that.'

Emery looked at her retreating figure, grimacing with the aftermath of the shock that had coursed through his body before he sat bolt upright with the realisation. The abbreviation BEG at the end of Eliane's text was now clear to him. It stood for BIG EVIL GRIN.

He sighed. It was beginning already, Eliane getting her own way. He knew that she would continue to push her parents over everything. Then, one day, they wouldn't budge over something. And that would be the day when all hell would break loose.

He went downstairs where both sets of parents were having a glass of sherry. Both his mother and father were surprised to see him come down before he was ordered to.

He wanted to say something, to warn them, but he felt stupid and uncomfortable.

'Oh and by the way, your daughter is going to murder you in a few years time when you don't allow her to get her own way over something.'

Emery Dalton looked at Eliane's parents. He couldn't say anything, it was ridiculous.

Then he realised, it was going to have to be him.

A wave of optimism washed over him.

The End

Blood

Runs Cold

Monday October 3rd 2016

This is for me. I don't want anyone else discovering it.

I have decided to keep a journal. Why? I have no idea, but there is something wrong and things are changing so fast that I can't keep up. I am writing this at work and I do feel a little weight lifting already. My memory is sharp, so I can provide myself with a clear, detailed and accurate account when I read it back. I'm just going to write it as it happens at my leisure; when I'm alone. I hope I'm doing the right thing.

Tuesday October 4th 2016

Mr Thoughtfully Reliable I call him, my husband of seven years, Josh. It's the same every time he returns. I hear the key turn gently in the lock of our front door, and sure enough my faith in him is rewarded as he closes the door with admirable quietness. He always pauses, to take his shoes off, and hangs his suit jacket up before making his way lightly towards the bathroom. He closes the door carefully before switching on the light and I can hear him undressing, each item of clothing rustling quietly as he removes it. I count them through as a sort of game. That's his tie being undone and removed, his shirt, the belt buckle on his trousers is the most unmistakable single sound, before the swish of his suit trousers falling to the ground begins to provide images of quite a different sort. All this sensitivity so that he doesn't disturb me. Yet I am aware that all is not right, but I force that to the back of my mind and focus on the here and now.

I lie here in our bed thinking how grateful and lucky I am to have such a kind and considerate husband. Within a few minutes I hear him turn the shower on and the water jets start to splash. I'm almost tempted to leap out of bed and join him in there. But I won't, not again, not after last week.

I drift off into a daydream of sorts for a few moments before I realise that the shower has been turned off and I can no longer hear the hot water boiler. I wriggle in anticipation of Josh coming to bed, pleased to be safe in my arms again. It's as if I'm a sanctuary for him after his gruelling day at work. Of course, I allow him some latitude so he can 'wind-down.'

We don't want children. Josh made that very clear when he started getting serious. I can honestly say I wasn't bothered one way or the other really, although I don't think my mother was best pleased. But then we haven't spoken for years. She would have wanted grandchildren so that she could tell them what to do and they could tell her how much they loved her. She was an interfering busybody most of the time. Not a healthy relationship from my way of thinking. It was clear that she took an immediate dislike to Josh all those years ago, but then perhaps that was what I wanted and hoped for.

'How you doing, baby?'

Josh's body glistens in the murky light as he steps into our bedroom.

'I'm fine now you're home,' I say in a quiet, expectant tone.

Josh smiles at me in that way he has of looking dangerous. That always seems to provoke a little tingle of fear. And yet at the same time I can feel the desire in me rising. I glance casually at the digital clock on the bedside table. It shows a little before two. Josh catches my glance as he gets in beside me.

'No early start in the morning Penn. There's a sales rep meeting with the managers from half nine and that extends into a working lunch.'

My eyes grow wide in anticipation at what that means. I pull the duvet down so Josh can see what I'm wearing.

He gasps as his eyes trail over my body then he lowers his head and pushes my lips apart with his probing tongue. How thoughtful of him, he's shaved his stubble this time. Sometimes he returns home with a beard and doesn't shave on his return, as if he's pretending to be someone else. I respond with an ardour that only my Josh can satisfy.

Wednesday October 5th 2016

It was difficult leaving Josh in bed this morning, but we had time to make love again before I eventually got up and had a shower. I was at work just before a quarter to ten and found that Professor Johnson, my boss, was in a Heads of Department meeting all day, something about student numbers and falling revenue.

Josh told me that he might not be home until tomorrow night as there is some talk of the sales reps going out for dinner and maybe a club after. He'd stay in a hotel rather than disturb me for another night.

'I don't mind you disturbing me darling, when you bring me home such a lovely present.'

I fondled him and he began to go hard once more.

'No Penn it's not fair on you. I wouldn't normally bother with this but...well...there's word on the rumour mill that there's a manager's post in the offing so I thought I'd better do a little networking and see how the land lies.'

Oh my hard-working, caring soul of a husband.

We've been married for seven years. I was twenty one when I met him, Josh a decade older than me. I knew within hours of meeting him that he was the one for me and I think he felt that too. When he asked me to marry him after less than a year I burst into tears, I was so happy. We didn't have a lavish ceremony – just a couple of Josh's friends as witnesses, but I was so in love with him that I didn't care about the minutiae of how and where – just as long as we were married.

Josh doesn't get on with his parents. He's had no any contact with them for years. When I told my mother I was getting married she forbade me to do it. She told me not to ruin my life by marrying a womanising loser. I got cross and told her exactly what I was going to do. Suffice to say we haven't spoken for over seven years now, but I'm still married to the man I love so what should that tell her? She could be dead for all I know – or care.

The university grounds are dappled in warm sunshine as I stroll towards my parked Audi. It is a little after four thirty and my working day as PA to the Head of the Department of Biological Sciences is over. I love flexi time.

As I press the fob to open my car I notice a very fit looking, toned student running through the grounds, togged up in tight shorts and T shirt. He smiles broadly as he approaches me and I see his eyes roam all over me. It's a good feeling like bathing in sunshine. I pause at my car door, watching as he jogs away from me. He turns a couple of times as he does so. I begin to evaluate the possibilities.

◘

My mobile ring tone jingles into life and I am brought abruptly back to reality. Is it that time already? As I answer the call I look at the time and sure enough it is six o'clock, on the dot.

'Josh baby, where are you and how did the rep meeting go?'

'Where are you Penn? Still at work? At home? What are you wearing? Some short skirt again or tight trousers and a see-through blouse? Tell me now?'

I begin to shake at the ferocity of Josh's tone. You would think that I would be familiar and at ease with his...foibles, but this is more aggressive than usual. I know he's only like this because he loves me and cares for my well being, little love.

'I'm at home Josh. I finished work at four thirty, just as I said I would when you phoned at three. I'm wearing that black T shirt that you like with the low top and a pair of leggings. And yes I am on my own. I miss you baby.'

There is some sort of rustling coming from the end of the line before Josh responds.

'That's...good - I'll phone at nine.'

There is a breathlessness in his tone and more rustling before the call is terminated.

Josh is actually a doctor, a PhD doctor but he found pharmaceutical research boring and limiting. So after two years he moved into sales, which seems to agree better with him. When he was researching he'd come home frustrated and it took all my powers of persuasion to soothe and calm him. He's far more settled, happier and at ease with himself and the world these days. He's rarely on edge now.

He's told me on more than one occasion that he would get excited seeing me having sex with other men. I told him I would do it if he wanted me to but that I didn't think it would do much for me. He contradicted himself then by saying that maybe that wasn't such a good idea. It might turn him on in one way, but after the thrill had gone, he wasn't sure how he would react to seeing me in such a compromising position. He said he thought he might want to kill me! I said jokingly that if he had sex with another girl I would want to kill her and him and...I wouldn't want to watch because I'd want to take her place. I could see that this type of talk was getting him very excited...although I was a little uncomfortable...but as I said that, he...well it didn't last very long.

I got home and worked out on the cross trainer for forty five minutes before having a cool shower. I ate a small pasta meal with a side salad washed it down with half a litre of chilled water. I glanced at my mobile. Josh would be phoning in twenty five minutes. I quietly hoped he hadn't had more than a couple of drinks. I went upstairs and let my robe fall to the floor. My clothes were laid out on the bed and I cast my eye over them once more to confirm they were appropriate. Oh yes. After Josh's call I was going out.

◘

9. 20 pm

My writing is spidery. I can barely hold the pen. I am shaking so much.

Josh had been drinking when I answered his call dead on nine. He was agitated and spoiling for a fight the moment I opened my mouth, to the extent that I was relieved that there was a distance between us.

'What are you wearing whore?' Josh spat the words out with a vehemence I hadn't experienced from him before. I tried to reply as calmly and evenly as I could.

'I've just had a shower my darling. Now I'm sitting on the edge of the bed wearing my short bathrobe, wishing you were here, baby.'

'Liar. You're strutting your shit around dressed up, showing your tits off, with a skirt so short it barely covers your ass.'

'You must be wishing you were here too baby with me dressed up for you like that, but you're not, so I am wearing my bath robe.'

'You fucking slut, why would I want you to dress up for me, ever?!'

Josh had never spoken to me in THAT way before. Why would he do that now? Maybe the vacancy for the manager's role is out of his grasp or beyond him in some way. maybe he's having a hard time accepting it. I decided to steer the conversation that way.

'Have there been any developments on the manager's role darling?'

'Nothing yet, just a few little pointers. It's still all up in the air.'

It appeared that the change of tack had calmed him down.

'So you're still in with a chance?'

There was a delay of some seconds before he replied, as though he were distracted by something at his end of the phone.

'Yes, yes all still to play for...well you must be tired Penn so I'll let you run. I'll be home tomorrow night...sometime.'

And he was gone. I stared at the mobile in my hand for a good thirty seconds. What had that been about? Normally if he'd had a couple of drinks a little flirting could quickly lead into phone sex, which was provocative but playful, not like the bile he had just spat at me. I dropped the phone on the bed and began to dress.

God I AM going to enjoy myself to night.

Thursday 6th October 2016

His name is Cody and he is twenty. He told me he had seen me a couple of times walking through the grounds of the university, but had always shied away from approaching me because of the band of gold. He felt uncomfortable coming on to a married woman even though she might seem to flirt and encourage him. I told him it was alright as I'd approached him, so conscience absolved!

54

We met in the student bar at nine thirty. We had one drink together, mine iced water with lemon and lime, before we slipped out together a little after ten. As we strapped ourselves in to my Audi a3 convertible I glanced to my left and felt a tingle up my spine at the tightness of the seat beat across his chest.

'Wow, slick wheels.'

'They are aren't they? Now sit back and relax. We have a little drive before us.'

'Little? How far is little?'

'The Excelsior Hotel in York. I've booked a room.'

'But that's sixty miles away.'

'Have you got to be up early in the morning?'

'Well, no but...'

'Am I not worth the journey?'

Before Cody could reply I leaned over, placed my hand on his inner thigh and gently kissed him on the mouth. As I pulled away Cody smiled.

'Yes, of course you are. I'm sorry, let's get going.'

I glanced nonchalantly at my hand still on his thigh and gently caressed his leg moving inwards a little before looking up at him. I smiled and started the car. I like younger men, they are so malleable, so willing to please.

◘

Thank god for flexi-time! Professor Johnson, Maurice, is such a laid back, easy going guy, especially for a senior academic. He greeted me with a wide smile as I waltzed into his office just before ten this morning.

'Good morning Mrs Styles I've left a copy of my itinerary for today and tomorrow on your desk. You are aware that you'll be accompanying me to the Grants Select Committee this afternoon aren't you?'

'I am Professor, to record the minutes.'

'That is correct. Then if you would print those out to disseminate to the members of the Biology Academic Board Committee for next Monday.'

'Very good Professor. Will you require me for that meeting as well?'

Maurice Johnson looked at me with a crinkling of his furrows.

'I'll establish whether that will be necessary and let you know.'

'Very well Professor.'

He looked at me again, this time with a slightly more concerned air.

'Mrs Styles I hope you don't mind my commenting, but you do look a little tired. I trust the workload is not getting too much for you?'

I laughed in what I hoped would sound like an appreciative, dismissive manner.

'No, not at all Professor. Last night my husband Josh didn't return home until four in the morning. He'd been away with work again, so my sleep has been a little disrupted.'

'I didn't mean to pry. Just noting a little concern for the well-being of my staff.'

'Thank you, that's very thoughtful, but I assure you there is no cause for concern. I'm fine.'

He appeared content with my explanation and left the room, allowing me to get a strong cup of coffee before I started my work. That, however, proved less straightforward than usual as I struggled to focus after the night's events. I had managed to crawl into my bed at a little after five. After four hours sleep I got up and persuaded myself, reluctantly, to go for a very short, but brisk run. I followed that with some exercises and stretches which rejuvenated me. After a couple of hot and cold showers I didn't feel too bad. 'Burning the candles at both ends,' my father would have said.

I'm smiling now at the recollection of him. I always got on better with Dad than with my mother. But he died when I was twelve and, me being an only child, my mother focussed all her energies on me. That's something Josh and I have in common.

My thoughts turn towards my husband and his return. His assertion that he'll be home 'sometime' tonight could mean anytime from early evening to the early hours, I never know for sure. Take last night. I knew he had been in the north east for the last couple of days around Ripon or Thirsk. He had a company car, an Audi A5 Coupe which I know he loves driving. He has had the new one for about two months, but I've only driven it once, while mine was in the garage for a service.

When I opened the glove compartment I found many packets of condoms, but that paled against what I found in the boot when I loaded the shopping. There was all manner of disposable clothing; a mixture of white and blue – boiler suits; caps; gloves and overshoes. Why did he have all this stuff?

I asked him, as casually as I could later the same evening.

'All that stuff Penn? It's simple really. Some of the labs and research places I visit have a quarantine and contamination policy so I put all that garb on when I enter some of the units to minimise the risk of contagions.'

Well, that sounded plausible to me so I didn't probe any further. I forgot to mention the condoms.

As the day wore on my tiredness began to catch up with me although a pasta salad lunch and a walk through the grounds kept it at bay. The minutes of the Grant Select Committee are not the most stimulating agenda to have to record, but I managed to concentrate enough that I didn't miss anything. That meeting lasted a little under two hours so I didn't return to my office until nearly four o'clock to discover that I had missed five phone calls from Josh, the first of them at nine that morning.

'Fuck,' I said aloud to no one.

On other occasions when Josh has been unable to make contact it has taken all my powers to convince him of my fidelity. Josh doesn't seem to process the fact that I can't always take his calls, often for long periods of time. Oh well, I was going to have to exercise those skills again. I am after all a past master, or should that be mistress? I'm not scared of Josh. I know that face to face I can melt and mould him out of any angry suspicions into something more pliant, devoted and humble.

But that said, there is something about him that changes when he isn't at home around me. Scared is too strong a word, but certainly I am more wary coming home at night, more on my guard about what I say, how I talk to him. Before yesterday though, he had never called me unpleasant names. Perhaps I was over reacting though. Maybe it was down to the pressure he has put himself under to want to better himself by getting the manager's position.

58

I was thinking about this while I opened a document and began typing up the minutes of the Grants Select Committee meeting. After I'd recorded the headings, who had attended and the items up for discussion I found my focus wavering. I glanced hopefully at the clock on the computer. It was almost four thirty. I glanced at the pages of minutes I had taken and decided on a place I would get to before I stopped. I would complete the rest of it tomorrow. Even typing slower I still made more errors than I would normally. Correcting them slowed me down even further.

I was still distracted by thoughts of the names Josh had called me and what I was going to do and how I was going to play this evening when he returned. It would be an advantage if I knew when he would return but he never phones, just turns up out of nowhere. If he is going to be later than nine he will at least phone me then, but apart from that I am left to drift.

Usually I'll prepare dinner in case he is home around seven, something that won't spoil if he is a lot later. I come home and have a session on the cross trainer and do some yoga before showering and making myself presentable. Then I wait for my prince to arrive. That's how it'll be tonight.

◘

10.20 pm

I've not seen him like this before. He's like a caged animal ensnared in a trap with no means of escape. He used to be like this before he moved into sales, only he's deeper in the abyss this time. The one thing I can be certain of is that he has no chance of landing the manager's post, judging from his monosyllabic replies to my gentle queries. I put this melancholy down to Josh's disappointment, but console myself with the thought that he'll find his way out of whatever he is caught in, in his own good time.

Josh returned home at almost eight thirty and without a word to me made straight for the bathroom. Within seconds I could hear the shower running. I busied myself by getting dinner prepared and laid out, but he didn't emerge to join me until almost an hour later. I noticed, with some revulsion, that he hadn't shaved and the prickly growth was somewhere between stubble and a beard. Ugggh! But I would gain nothing by bringing it up so I held my tongue.

He sat down at the table, still mute and with downcast eyes, unwilling or unable to meet my own. He began eating, forking mouthfuls like an automaton. His eyes were glazed over as if his mind were lost in some deep inner recess trapped with his thoughts.

'You seem pre-occupied baby, have you had a tough day?'

I decided to risk initiating conversation, despite my foreboding.

He glanced up from his plate and looked, as though he couldn't see who had addressed him. After a few seconds his head nodded a few times before he resumed his methodical consumption of his meal.

We finished eating in silence. While I washed up the crockery and cutlery, Josh sat at the table still deep in thought. I walked up to him, stood to one side and lay my hand on the back of his, grasping it, encouraging him to his feet. He did so without resistance and I led him slowly to the sofa in the lounge where we both sat down.

'Do you want to tell me about your trip baby?'

He looked sideways at me with an expression I found difficult to interpret.

'No,' he whispered.

'Is it about the manager's job?'

He nodded and whispered, 'they're broken.'

I had no idea what he meant and so carried on talking about the vacancy.

'Is that what this is all about? Because if it is the job baby, it doesn't matter, it really doesn't matter. You don't need to prove anything to me.'

He looked in my face once again without indicating whether I was correct or not. We sat like this for I don't know how long before Josh punctured the silence, his voice cracking with emotion.

'I only want love, that's not too much to expect is it?'

I covered his hand with mine but before I could whisper any sweet replies he continued, his voice stronger than before.

'I don't want to do it, but they leave me with no choice. They shouldn't do that.'

And those were the final words he said to me before standing up abruptly and going to bed.

I allowed him some space and wrote up the diary for half an hour, confident of being left undisturbed, before making a camomile tea.

Friday 7th October 2016

I'm awake very early. This is all getting way too scary. Josh is at home and he's freaking me out. I've no time to myself, so I'm going to say I've got to go into work. Oh God - he's coming, I've got to g...

61

Tuesday 11th October

I haven't had the opportunity to write this up after Friday.

Josh was asleep when I went into the bedroom after finishing my camomile tea. I slipped in beside him and hardly dared to breathe for fear of waking him. I hoped that a good night's sleep might help his mood, although I had no idea what his timetable for Friday was. I soon found out.

On waking it was clear that his disposition towards me was unchanged. He was sullen, disagreeable and still generally monosyllabic. He took no pleasure in telling me that he wasn't in work today. He was furious when I told him that I had to go to work and he badgered me to stay at home with him. To do what, I ask myself? So that he could frighten me even more with his morose behaviour? At one point I did fear that he might actually prevent me from leaving the house, but he stopped short of doing that. Not only did I go in to work but for once I was early, grateful for the chance to escape from the prison that was my home.

I visibly relaxed on leaving the house and did not turn to wave goodbye, although I knew he was watching me leave. This was killing me. I couldn't talk to him, at least not in any meaningful way that got through to him. I did not know what to do.

As nine o'clock approached I kept glancing at my mobile standing upright against the window, waiting for his military precision phone call. It didn't arrive. My relief was tempered by my worrying about whether I would pay for that later. He might blame me.

Professor Johnson came to my rescue as I was on the brink of descending into a pit of my own.

'Mrs Styles, I'll leave my itinerary for next week on your desk. I would like you to accompany me to the Biology Academic Board meeting on Monday for the whole day.'

He paused, a little unsure of what he was going to say and how to say it.

'I was wondering whether you would feel able to take on some, perhaps more interesting duties? I have a high regard for your work ethic Mrs Styles, and was looking to you to deputise for myself at some of the meetings I find myself having to attend with monotonous regularity. They would all be within your capabilities, so do not worry on that account. There would be an associated remuneration package. I wouldn't expect you to take this on at your current salary level.'

I was taken aback for a moment.

'Thank you very much for considering me, Professor.'

'You know how it all works Mrs Styles, you would blend in seamlessly.'

'Then I accept your offer, Professor Johnson.'

He smiled warmly and I felt grateful towards him for providing a little light in my darkness.

'Your current hours and structure of working will continue as before. I see no reason to change those. Shall we say from Monday?'

'Thank you. I look forward to it.'

'Believe me when I say that you will be helping.'

He turned and walked away into his office, leaving the door between us open.

That had been a turn up for the books. With that glow providing some comfort I returned to Josh and what I was going to do. I decided that if I could engage him in conversation I would try and gently probe what it was that was bothering him. Maybe that would best be served away from home. As it was, events took all control away from me.

◻

I got home a little after five thirty, my pleasure at my promotion and increase in salary resulting in me staying later than I usually did. Perhaps that was my showing Professor Johnson that I was willing to handle the responsibility.

Josh was still quiet and reflective, but he had gone to the gym for two hours, swam a few lengths and spent some time in the health suite having a sauna and a session in the steam room and spa, so his temper had modified into something less confrontational.

We talked in general terms about things, nothing specific, but I tactfully refrained from mentioning my promotion.

I knew he was feeling better, perhaps a little contrite even, because he had made dinner, chilli with pitta bread.

On my arrival he had greeted me almost normally, but there was no questioning why I was so late, nor any aggressive stance at all. I wasn't naive enough to believe that all had been resolved, though.

We sat down on the sofa together and had the chilli on trays, watching the six o'clock news. The first story was the continuing fallout and consequences of the Brexit vote, while the second item was the US Presidential election.

The third story in was from North Yorkshire. A girl, Rachelle Temple, had been raped and left for dead, only to somehow miraculously survive. The report continued that Rachelle had only been able to provide fragmentary details of the attack itself and a scant description of her assailant. The officer in charge of the case, a DCI Raice Steadman asked for help from the public in this depraved, evil crime.

'We know that Rachelle Temple left Hambelton Leisure Centre a little after six o'clock in the evening due to CCTV footage. There is then a large gap until twenty five past ten, almost four and a half hours later, when despite her life threatening injuries she managed to reach a secluded cottage on the outskirts of the Cleveland Hills and raise the alarm. We would like to speak to anyone who can provide sightings or knowledge of Rachelle's movements between six pm and ten twenty five. As far as the doctors have told us Rachelle remains in a critical although stable condition.'

Josh blanched when the item came up. He sat riveted to the screen his fork held in mid-air, chilli dropping onto his plate.

I sat back in the sofa as a cold sensation passed through me. Could Josh be having an affair? Maybe he's met someone else and wants to be with her and not me? Why would he have condoms in the car?

Maybe this 'mood' he was in was nothing to do with the manager's job, maybe it was all to do with him being unhappy with me, wanting to leave me for someone else that he's met on his travels? There were so many questions and so few answers. It was infuriating!

Don't be so stupid Penn! You know Josh loves you and wouldn't want to come home to anyone else - and why wouldn't he? You do anything and everything that he asks of you. No...no, he wouldn't leave me, there's no need. He has everything he wants, meaning his own way. No. You don't need to go down this road. Josh isn't like that. He is your husband and look what he sacrificed to be with you, any form of relationship with his parents. No...no, there's nothing for you to get upset or concerned about. He has his moments to be sure, but underneath it all he is sensitive, gentle and kind. I know my man.

Still, it was something of a coincidence that he had been up there in North Yorkshire at the time that this attack took place and this nagged at the back of my mind. I ruminated for a moment and glanced up at him. He was as white as a sheet and sat, unmoving as though frozen.

Well, as I've said before, as long as he comes home to me...

'I'm scared Penn.'

I looked at him.

'I know. Did you do anything different? Did you take any short cuts? Anything that deviated from your normal routine.'

'No, I don't think so,' he was plaintive.

'You don't think so? This is your life and freedom at stake here, not to mention mine and you don't think so? You should know, one hundred percent. Anything less is opening you, us, up to risk and discovery. Did you do anything differently?'

'No,' he said stronger this time.

'That's alright then. Right. We need to sort this out Josh. Talk to me.'

He put a couple of forkfuls of chilli into his mouth, chewed them and then took a drink from the glass of water in front of him.

'I was disturbed, I don't know what by, but it made me jittery and I got careless.'

'If you haven't deviated from your routine and you left no evidence there'll be nothing to link you to her. You wore the balaclava?'

'Yes.'

'And didn't speak?'

'No.'

'Then the only type of description she can give is limited to your build, height, weight, maybe your smell.'

'I don't wear deodorant, you know that.'

'I meant body odour. I think you're worrying unnecessarily, and you've put me through hell. I thought it was the manager's job.'

'Oh that, no. I'm not bothered with that. And they still haven't made a decision yet anyway. I should hear any time.'

Here was my opportunity.

'Well, if you want omens, I was promoted on Thursday by Professor Johnson.'

Josh was silent and cast his head down.

'And I wasn't there for you to share the news with because I was so wrapped up in my problems.'

'Oh baby, it's okay, we can celebrate over the weekend, maybe go away for a couple of days.'

I stood and moved around to his side and cradled his head. His arm circled my waist and we stayed like that for a moment. I sat down again and we both finished our chilli.

'Thank you Josh, that was delicious.'

As I looked at him a wave of recognition washed over me as a thought entered my head. It was all so obvious when I actually thought about it. All those clichés and sayings about couples mingled in my head; a problem shared is a problem halved; don't settle for a relationship that doesn't allow you to be yourself; couples that travel together, stay together.

They say opposites attract, but I don't believe that for a moment. It's great sharing an interest, it brings us so much closer, *a folie a deux* as the French say.

I stood up, feeling a wash of confidence flow over me, smiling as I did so. Yes, I reminded myself as I picked up the remote, you do anything and everything for him, don't you? The TV screen was showing a face I recognised now. It had only been last night. I smiled and felt a warm, comforting glow. I looked at Josh and smiled.

A student, a boy, coming on to me, a happily married woman, as if I was a piece of meat. I turned the TV off. Josh and I had more talking to do. Away from home and all its associated pressures would be best.

I'll leave the journal at home for the weekend and let him read it after we return. Then, maybe, we can keep one between us.

The End

The
Bare Bones

There was a buzzing, like a fly in his ear that would not go away. Kris Tunnicliffe's eyes barely opened at first but then the reason he had set his alarm hit him. He reached out a large muscular arm to silence the grating noise. 3.00am. He switched on his bedside lamp.

He slid out of bed and made his way to the kitchen of his one bedroom flat. He reached inside the fridge without looking and brought out a plastic drink container with a pink liquid colouring almost three quarters of its capacity. He snapped open the mouthpiece cap, lifted it to his lips, and began to slurp it down, hardly pausing for breath. He drank half of it in one draught, before moving to the kitchen table to check his daily health plan for the day ahead.

His eyes scrolled down; all the details of his diet, what he was going to eat and when, the times he was going to consume the protein shakes and other supplements he took during the day and night, as well as the weights and reps regime he would follow. He wasn't in work until ten in the morning, but he would have to work until six thirty. That meant he would go to the gym first thing for a couple of hours and then return after work, twelve hours later. He replaced the sheet of paper on the table, finished the protein shake and made his way back to bed.

He remained sitting up, wide awake, casting an eye around the room. His eyes were drawn to the framed photograph next to the lamp. He didn't know why he kept it so close. It always reminded him and sent him into a dark place. He dismissed his sentimentality and checked his phone. There was a text message and a voicemail from his older brother, Jeff. That would be his mother's doing. He returned the phone to his bedside table and looked at the clock. It was almost three fifteen. He gazed vacantly around his bedroom, his mind swimming with the doubts and insecurities that plagued him.

He'd had another dream. He couldn't remember the details but he knew, somehow, that it was linked to the bodybuilding competition he had entered. It was less than three months away and he wasn't ready, that was the bottom line. He was doing everything he could to be in peak condition. He had increased the amount of time he spent in the gym; apart from work that was all he was doing with his life. He had increased the number and quality of the reps, taken more and better quality shakes and supplements and been strict about his diet, but it had failed. The definition, symmetry and proportion he needed were eluding him.

When a couple of the other guys had told him he looked good and that he was pushing himself too much, he had ignored them. What did they know? He hadn't spoken to them since, in fact he didn't really talk to anyone in the gym anymore. He preferred to focus all his time and attention on honing his body.

As the thought of work filtered back into his head he grimaced and laid his head back on the pillow, hoping that thoughts of his mundane job would send him back to sleep for a few hours.

He was a Civil Enforcement Officer patrolling the streets around Rilford, checking up on motorists, parking and traffic violations. The dullness of the job was only marginally brightened by his willingness to engage motorists in confrontation and arguments. He knew very well that he used his physicality as an intimidation. By adopting a threatening posture and attitude he invited the perpetrator to 'have a go.' That invitation had never been taken up, although he lived in hope. In truth, he lived for developing his physique to the point of perfection, nothing else mattered. But it paid enough for him to afford the flat and the bodybuilding lifestyle that he desired.

He glanced nonchalantly around the bedroom, his eyes now accustomed to the hazy gloom the 40W light bulb provided. He noted the bench and sets of weights in the corner, the pile of bodybuilding magazines stacked by the side of the wardrobe and the many plastic containers filled with pills and powders. Then his eyes drifted to the boxes filled with glass vials carefully piled up on the desk.

He had to win, nothing else mattered. He had few friends and hardly ever went out, unless Jeff was in the country and talked him into going out for a beer. But he wouldn't do that now, not with the competition so close. He'd sacrificed every other part of his life to pursue this dream, but he knew it would all be worth it, if he won. Unable to sleep, he got out of bed again and stood in front of the full length mirror, throwing poses and postures.

Mirror mirror on the wall

Who's the buffest of them all?

He held an angled pose, scrutinizing his frame. When he had begun training for the competition some nine months earlier he had compared himself to the others in the gym. At first he was a little behind but soon noted that he had overtaken all of them in his dedication and commitment. Now he knew he had taken a major step backwards. He wasn't going to be ready in time. The guys in the competition were going to be the best in their respective gyms.

He looked at his physique with a critical eye, like a judge would do in three months time. He sighed heavily, resigned to what he saw; poor definition, asymmetrical muscle groups and no muscle proportion. He had to work harder, push himself to the limit, nothing else would be enough. God, it made him so mad, so frustrated. Then a thought that made him smile entered his head. After a punishing session in the gym, he'd take his frustrations out on those bastard drivers. The idea elevated him and his roving eye caught the boxes on the desk. He broke his pose and picked up a syringe lying on top of the boxes.

⌂

'But I've still got three minutes before the time runs out.'

Kris smiled broadly, but there was no humour in his eyes.

'I can't see the time because the ticket is not stuck on the windscreen.' He continued writing out the parking ticket.

'But it's only fallen off and landed on the top of the dashboard. Look - you can see it if you crane your neck around a bit.'

The man in his sixties was becoming exasperated. That had been Kris's intention, although it seemed unlikely that this would deteriorate much further, more was the pity.

'I can't adopt that position because of health and safety,' said Kris as he fixed the notice under the windscreen wiper.

The man laughed out loud.

'A bloke built like a brick shithouse like you can't turn his head a bit to read the time. You're a bit of a pussy my son, you need to develop a backbone.'

Kris slowly turned his head and fixed his eyes on the man, who at five seven or so was a good eight inches shorter than him.

'Would you like to help me develop that backbone, old man?'

'There's no need for hostility.'

The man removed the notice from the windscreen, unlocked the car door and started the car. He gave Kris a quick sidelong glance before pulling away from the space and driving off.

Kris smiled once more, still without humour.

'Wanker,' he said aloud to no one.

He glanced around the car park and made a decision, taking out his mobile from an inner jacket pocket. It was only half two. God, the day was passing by like a snail moving in treacle.

He hadn't been able to return to sleep. He had been up and about a little after half five which meant he had had a damn good breakfast and still been at the gym before it opened. He put in a strenuous two hour session, and felt all the better for it. He exchanged a nod of the head to one or two of his fellow gym enthusiasts, but hadn't talked to any of them. He'd eaten again and taken some supplements, but then his mood had nosedived at the thought of wandering around town for eight hours. Even the possibility of taking out his aggravation on the drivers barely registered. He'd had a few heated exchanges with motorists, one threatening to report him, another telling him he was a little bully, a jobsworth, but it was all water off a duck's back to Kris.

He returned to the here and now and checked how many violations and tickets he had awarded. He smiled at his use of that word. It sounded like a reward or a prize earned through a good deed or word. Nothing could be further from the truth. He had always been well aware that no one he came across thought positively about what he did. He didn't give a shit. He'd hand out the ticket and if they didn't like it they could appeal. He glanced down at the count for the day. He was doing ok. That should keep his supervisor off his back if he maintained that number for the rest of his shift. He felt in one of his jacket pockets and brought out a plastic vial filled with pills. He opened it with his large, muscular fingers and popped two pills in his mouth, allowing them to dissolve on his tongue. He'd take a slow walk back to his car and have another protein shake, then continue by checking that small, private car park that always seemed to attract drivers trying to get out of paying.

As he took a step forward he felt a strange, detached sensation wash over him. He reached out a hand and let it rest on a car boot to steady himself. He felt giddy and light headed, small flashing lights before his eyes. He put his hand-held device into its pocket on his vest and rubbed his eyes with his balled fists. Opening them again for a fleeting moment, Kris thought he saw a skeleton dancing as though it were a puppet on strings. He felt faint and nauseous. Then it was gone and the young man ambling through the car park turned towards him with an unfriendly air. He stood up straight and looked around. No one else had observed his 'little turn.' What the hell was that all about? He hadn't had one of those episodes for at least a week. Bugger. Oh well, he felt fine now. He pulled his vest down straight, removed the device from its pocket and set off for the private car park.

⌂

The row of six bodybuilders stood in a variety of poses showing off their shape and contours to best advantage. The line of judges beneath them scrutinized each and every one with a clear, focussed eye.

From out of the curtain at the side of the stage came Kris Tunnicliffe, or at least a version of him. This version was six inches shorter and twenty kilograms lighter with a puny, sixty kilogram body. The audience erupted into laughter and even the judges' faces creased into smiles at the pathetic specimen who dared to come onto this stage in such exalted company.

Undeterred, he began striking poses and holding them as though he had something to show off. His peers all leant forward and looked down the line at this usurper, this pretender, who clearly had no idea what he was doing.

As he maintained the postures a metamorphosis took place and a more athletic, muscular, correctly proportioned Kris Tunnicliffe appeared. But as he demonstrated his

75

prowess his skin began to peel away in layers, from the top of his skull, across his face and onto his torso and arms. Like a tide it worked its way down the length of his whole body revealing the muscle groups, like an anatomy textbook. He carried on his moves oblivious to anything else occurring.

Kris sat up in bed sweating, eyes and mouth wide open in fear. What the hell had that been about? He looked around in the darkness making sure of his surroundings. It was ok, he was in his bedroom and not on the stage. He took a deep breath and looked at the bedside clock. It was ten minutes to two. His alarm would be going off in a little over an hour anyway. He turned on the bedside lamp, changed the alarm to half past six and stared at that photograph again. It was the only memento he had allowed himself to keep. Maybe that was why it was still here, because it was the only link to that part of his past. He shook his head as if to dislodge those thoughts, then he placed the photo frame face down, and got out of bed and went to the toilet.

He had had a good session in the gym after work and this had rescued him from the trauma of the working day. With the competition getting ever closer, he had decided to start the cutting phase of his diet where he began lowering the amount of calories he consumed. This was to ensure that his body was lean and carried little fat. He had turkey, with mixed vegetables and a jacket potato for dinner.

After dinner he thought about phoning his brother, Jeff, but he couldn't quite force himself to do it. He knew exactly how the conversation would pan out; the same way it always did.

'Kris, hi. Mum's asked me to call you because she's worried she hasn't seen you much. She needs to hear you tell her that you're fine and not pushing yourself to extremes. You know she's only worried about you buddy, so don't take it as us checking up on you. Be good

76

to hear from you. I know you've got that comp in a few months time, but take a bit of time out and give Mum a call. Ok?'

'Yeah sure Jeff. Tell Mum I'll phone in a few days.'

'Ok buddy, thanks for that, Mum will be relieved. Talk to you later. Bye Kris.'

'Bye Jeff.'

And that would be that until the next time Jeff called him, perhaps a little more irate because he hadn't phoned Mum in the meantime.

He opened the fridge door and drained half the protein shake. So now he had started having nightmares and seeing things. That skeleton in the car park; what was that? Was it an hallucination? The nightmare had felt real, as if he was living it, actually being within it, then remembering it vividly afterwards. He drank the rest of the shake, dropped the container in the sink and walked back to his room, trembling. He mustn't let this get to him.

He looked around his bedroom, not wanting to acknowledge what he wanted to do. No, he must try to cut the injections down. He was too reliant on them. His eyes were drawn to the photograph and he recoiled at the memories and turned the picture face down.

He got under the duvet and turned out the light, staring vacantly into the darkness.

He was still in that position when his alarm went off at half past six.

⌂

Kris watched his body carefully as his muscles contracted. A small voice in his head said,

'The mirror never lies.'

77

He threw a front double biceps and rotated his body to the left and right, slightly changing the point of view.

He was on a half day and after working from half past seven until one he had immediately gone to the gym. Lunchtimes were generally quieter and today was no exception. He had decided to really push himself and then take some time to analyse his body. He remained disappointed. That voice spoke in his head again.

What truth lies within a reflection in a mirror?

He stared into his own eyes, lost within himself. There were those who believed that training in front of a mirror would seriously affect your lifting in a negative way. But there was also a school of thought that debunked that. Kris used to enjoy watching himself lifting, especially if he caught others watching him in awe. But recently, probably because he was becoming less impressed with how he looked, he didn't enjoy it as much. He certainly didn't want anyone watching him. He knew he had become far too self conscious that he wasn't cutting the mustard anymore.

He clenched his fists and tucked them into the side of his abdomen, taking on a front lateral spread. He closed his eyes in concentration, then jumped, just half a step, as a macabre skeleton appeared in his mind's eye, flesh hanging from its bones. The skeleton stared back at him. Then it was gone. Despite the mirrors surrounding him, Kris rotated his body and scanned the gym to check whether anyone else had seen what had happened. The three other people he could see were all engaged in their own pursuits with their backs to him, two on bikes and the third on a treadmill. He turned back to see his own reflection gazing back at him with a haunting, heavy lidded aspect.

He looked almost asleep. He knew that by taking a protein shake in the early hours his sleep patterns would be disturbed, but he woke after the nightmare last night and didn't go back to sleep. Maybe he needed to get more sleep, he didn't look good. The little voice inside his head came to the rescue.

If it was easy to achieve everyone would do it. No pain, no gain.

He stared into his own eyes and forced himself to open them wider. There, that was better. He just needed to work himself harder, that was the answer. He'd been resting on his laurels, taking it easy, thinking it was all going to fall into his lap because he wanted it to. You didn't win competitions with thinking like that. Dedication and hard work, there was no substitute.

He turned his back to the mirror and threw a back lateral spread, before glancing over his right shoulder at his reflected image. He sighed heavily and dropped the pose. It was no use. He looked pathetic. He wouldn't get anywhere looking like this. He gritted his teeth and felt a wave of anger wash through him. You're just going to have knuckle down, stop feeling so sorry for yourself and work harder, he thought to himself. He'd beast it up and bulk up by doing more sets and reps. This was just his personal abyss, that was all. And when he conquered that, well it was all under his control again wasn't it?

Kris returned to the barbell and weights.

⌂

There was a buzzing in his ear, like a bee that wouldn't go away. Kris vaguely opened his eyes to find that his darkened bedroom was being illuminated from his bedside table. Without conscious thought he reached out to take the call.

'Kris, it's about fucking time.'

The welcoming tones of his elder brother, Jeff, stirring him from his cosseted place of refuge.

'Huhh Jeff, long time no...'

'Cut the bollocks Kris, this is not the time. Mum's died.'

Kris raised himself higher on his elbow.

'What? When? How? Why didn't you...'

'I fucking did, a few days ago. I left you a text and a voicemail telling you Mum had been taken into hospital and that she was really ill. But as usual you have your head so stuck up your buffed bodybuilding ass that you carry on your merry way because everything's hunky dory in Kris's macho posing world and fuck everyone else.'

Kris's shoulders sagged forward and his head hung a little lower. Jeff though had not finished.

'And while I'm at it, if you haven't bothered with Mum, I don't suppose you've been to the graves for months either have you? Stupid question. You need to come down from Olympus and live in the real mortal world, Kris. You're only half an hour from Mum yet it's me, thousands of miles away, who tells you what is happening with her. I don't give a shit that you don't call and talk to me but your mother? Well, it's too fucking late now. I'm flying back in the next forty eight hours to sort mum's funeral and the will. I'll let you know when and where it is, if you can be half assed to turn up.'

The line went dead.

Kris remained in that position, as though frozen, for a couple of minutes. He saw his mother with him and Jeff at the seaside somewhere just after their father had walked out. He thought it was Clacton, but wasn't sure. He'd have been eight or so at the time.

Then he remembered his mother coming up to the school because he'd had a fight and nearly killed a boy. He was sixteen and Jeff had left school and gone to college. Without his older brother some of the boys had decided to provoke 'Tunny' about his mother's reputation. One boy in particular, Ralph Chalmers, had goaded Kris until he snapped. Not a good move. Kris was already six feet tall and had been working out for a couple of months.

'What did you call my mother, you little piece of shit?'

Kris recalled the glimmer of fear in Chalmers' eyes, which steeled him.

'Not so gobby now are we Judith?'

 Kris had used Chalmers nickname without understanding its meaning, but it undermined Chalmers initial bravado further. He began backing away, but Kris followed him, advancing upon him like a bear. Chalmers cowardice in the face of a physical assault, after mouthing off at him from a distance at the start, made Kris see red. The mist came down and he landed three massive punches so quickly that Chalmers was already falling to the ground after the first. He leant over the prone figure of Chalmers as the chants of 'fight, fight' began to subside.

'That'll teach you to call my mother names, you fucking asshole.'

The other boys, possibly out of fear, backed up Kris's story of provocation (with the actual words Chalmers had used), and it was their confirmation that saved him from expulsion.

That turned out to be a turning point in Kris's life. From then on he asserted his physical self onto any situation and was prepared and willing to back it up.

He returned to the present and angrily switched his phone off, before glancing at the clock as he returned it to the table. It was a quarter to one. He'd had an early night and now that would be wasted. Fuck Jeff. Fuck his mother for dying. No, he didn't mean that. He got back under the duvet and lay there staring at the ceiling.

He'd admired his mother for the way she adapted to their father walking out on them. There were rumours about how she went about earning some of the money she got but he never saw any evidence to back them up. He knew she worked four days a week in the local market and then two days cleaning some large house near where they lived. Those jobs apart, he never bore witness to anything else. He and Jeff had talked about it back along, but Jeff was adamant that their mother had never, ever been on the game. Not that it would have mattered to him even if she had been, she was his mother. And now she was gone and he had been too preoccupied with himself to see her before she went. He didn't kid himself that his presence alone would have prevented her death, but he could have been there to say goodbye, and thanks. For only the second time since he was a child, Kris Tunnicliffe shed tears.

◊

His mother was pointing her finger at him. A large bony finger, devoid of skin, denuded of almost all tissue except for a few, dangling remnants. He didn't want to look – it would mean he had to acknowledge her face - but he was forced to confront it as it loomed large in his imagination, grotesque and macabre.

As soon as their eyes met a toothless, grin spread across her hag-like face.

'It's your fault I'm dead,' she lisped.

'No it's not,' he heard his voice protesting from out of the darkness, although his tone was reedy and strained as if he wasn't quite convinced.

'You would have gone anyway whether I had seen you before or not.'

It sounded as though he was trying to reassure himself never mind anyone else.

'But you did kill us, you bastard and you're supposed to have loved us.'

Kris Tunnicliffe fell out of bed, landing heavily on the floor, his body shaking as though an earthquake were passing through him. He felt cold and yet was sweating profusely. He lay prone, as his conscious thoughts fought to get into the here and now, from wherever they had been.

In his mind's eye he recalled the accusing image he had fleetingly caught a glimpse of in his dream. He had glimpsed the bloody, mutilated corpse of a young woman, no more than twenty one or so, holding the lifeless bodies of two very young children and a baby in her broken, maimed arms. His face began to crease up as the remembered anguish washed over him.

'Gail,' he whispered, 'Lexxie, Trixie and Baylen, I'm so, so sorry.'

He adjusted his body and switched the lamp on before picking up the face down photograph. As he brought it close his eyes brimmed with tears.

The photograph had been taken on Clacton Pier on a bright, sunny, clear blue sky day five years earlier. The beaming smile of a young woman, dressed in white shorts and a blue bikini top shone in his eyes as she held onto the handle of a buggy and a set of double reins. Kris lifted his hand and stroked the images with his index finger, tears streaming down his grim set face like slow trickling waterfalls.

He had met Gail in a gym. He had been cocky and sure of himself, a false confidence built on his physical prowess. She made him question his assumptions and challenged his prejudices. She unnerved him, but in a good way. He knew that he had become a better human being for sharing his life with her. That changed after she was gone.

The twin girls, Lexxie and Trixie had been born a year and a half into the relationship, by which time they were already living together in a three bed flat. Gail had fallen pregnant again when the girls were just over two and Baylen was born when they were nearly three years old.

He had cut down his bodybuilding to a 'just keeping fit' level and had no inclination to do anymore. He loved being a father - doting on his children. He had asked Gail to marry him six months after Baylen was born and he had loved being married to her. Jeff was pleased for him and Gail; relieved as well, if truth be known, that he had found someone who he could relate to. Their mother had been overjoyed at being a grandmother. Those were the days when he used to see her every week.

Then the darkness began to grow around him as his thoughts took him to a place he did not want to go.

He still could not explain it to himself, never mind anyone else.

Baylen was a bouncing boy, a little under a year old when Kris decided to enter a bodybuilding competition. Whether his head had been turned by others in the gym or he felt he had to prove himself he had no idea. He was sure it wasn't because he had become bored of being a father and husband, but could find no explanation for his decision. He knew that if he had increased his gym sessions just a little Gail would have lived with that. But he didn't do that. He threw himself into it like a madman. The more he did the more he wanted to do and the more he wanted to do the more they argued. He became obsessed with achieving his aims and began to add supplements to his regime and then steroids and then, other stuff. He had little thought for anything else, it consumed him.

When he had heard the news he had crumpled onto the floor, shocked and numbed. In reality he had never really got up again. His mother commiserated with him on his devastating loss, as did Jeff. But their pity had no meaning, no relevance.

'Can you take the car into the garage Kris before I use it tomorrow? There's something funny about the brakes. They keep locking.'

He had been so focussed on himself and his sole desire to train. Gail's request had been erased as soon as she said it.

He gazed on the photograph before the image began to dissolve. He opened the drawer on the bedside table and put the photograph inside it, face down. He stood up and looked at himself in the mirror, before walking over to the boxes of glass vials on the desk. He picked up a syringe and a couple of vials. After he had done this he would write up his health plans for the next week. He needed to plan ahead, to stay ahead.

The End

Bundle
of Nerves

'Maya, have you seen my cigarettes?'

Tulia Braithwaite shouted the question from her bedroom.

Maya Golding poked her head out of her own room.

'I saw you with them in the kitchen - look on the table?'

Now it was Tulia's turn to stick her head out.

'Really? I don't remember leaving them there.' She skipped past Maya, into the kitchen. 'You're right, they're here.'

'There you go. Didn't I say yesterday when you couldn't remember eating the last two doughnuts?' You're getting senile.'

Tulia looked at Maya.

'I don't and I'm not sure whether I did or not.'

'Senile at twenty eight, it's such a shame.'

'And therefore five years younger than you so what does that say?'

Tulia stopped in the doorway of Maya's bedroom with a broad grin on her face. Maya glanced up at her and smiled.

'It means I've got more grey cells than you. I don't forget where I put things or that I've eaten stuff and then can't remember, even though I am half a decade older.'

'Yeah right.'

Tulia opened the packet of cigarettes and glanced inside. She did a double take and took another look, bringing them closer to her face.

'You haven't had a couple have you Maya? I'm sure there were more in here than this.'

Maya glanced up at Tulia again.

'Oh dear now she can't remember smoking some fags...it's a downward spiral you're on girl. No, I haven't taken any. You know I wouldn't smoke those cheap shitty ones.'

'Just asking, that's all. Oh well, must have smoked more than I thought.'

'You didn't take them to work did you?'

'You know I don't. I just don't remember leaving them on the kitchen table last night.'

Maya gave Tulia a lingering look before returning her attention to her mobile.

Tulia and Maya had been housemates for a little over two years. They had met at the retail outlet where they both worked and when Maya left they had stayed in touch. Tulia was now a senior sales assistant while Maya had returned to accountancy after completing her diploma.

They shared a bungalow in Whitchurch, a market town in Shropshire close to the Cheshire border. It was a quiet, relaxed neighbourhood, close to the Community Hospital.

'Are you home tonight or will you be staying at Mel-Anne's?'

Maya raised her eyes from the device.

'I'm at Mel's, after yoga. You have my permission to have an orgy without my interruption.'

Tulia smiled.

'Hrrrph. It will be the opposite...as well you know.'

'Do you miss him?'

'God no! He was getting clingy you know? I was finding it difficult to breathe sometimes.'

'Yeah - you said. It's the only thing to do if it's not working.'

'You and Mel still happy?'

'I think so. We're good for each other, mutually supportive and all that, so yeah we're good.'

'Do you fancy going to the cinema later in the week? I'm sure we could find something we'd both enjoy.'

'Ok, I'll check out what's on.'

'Nothing scary or spooky.'

'It's only a film, it's not real, Maya.'

'I know but I don't like films like that...sudden noises or jumps...and the music...'

'I'll steer clear of horror ones then.'

'Please do.'

Tulia giggled at her friend's fear.

'I dunno. You and things that go bump in the night!'

Maya looked at Tulia.

'Or the day. What was that DVD we watched? You had a cushion over your face for most of it. That guy was in it – you said he was gorgeous.' She thought for a moment, 'yeah Morgan, Jeffrey Dean Morgan.'

'*The Resident* with Hilary Swank. It's a shame when the good looking ones turn out to be total creeps.'

'You were absolutely wetting yourself.'

'I was not.'

Tulia looked at Maya and a smile rippled across her lips.

'They're just scary stories to give you the heebie-jeebies. It's not like that sort of thing happens in real life is it?'

◊

With Maya staying at Mel-Anne's overnight, Tulia had taken a hot shower while her dinner was warming in the oven. Her day on the shop floor had been a challenging one, with a number of staff missing through sickness or because of cut backs. Not only had she had to oversee the smooth running of the whole department, which was what she was paid to do, but she had had to serve customers when the queues became too long. For the most part, that strategy had been successful, although one or two customers were difficult. At least there was no damage. She had patted herself on the back for nipping trouble firmly in the bud.

Now she was glad to have the night to herself. It would have been fine if Maya had been there, but with the amount of smiling, exchanging pleasantries and dealing with a couple of morons she had had to endure, a little time and space to herself was perfect.

After dinner she scrolled through the TV guide. Most reality TV left her cold and she found it difficult to understand why programmes featuring so called celebrities (and what did that mean in any case?) were so popular. There was nothing she wanted to watch so instead she looked through the DVD collection she and Maya had formed over the years. She put all the horror, thriller and action stuff to one side. She wanted something light, but that didn't mean rom-coms or girly movies – unless it was something like *Thelma and Louise*. No, tonight she was in the mood for something unchallenging. There it was; *Kung Fu Panda 2*. Perfect. She put it on and lost herself in the silliness of it all.

The film finished a little before ten so she watched the news and got ready for bed. She might have an equally testing day tomorrow. She thought about the missing cigarettes and the forgotten doughnuts while she brushed her teeth, but they faded from her mind as she picked up the book she was reading, *Wolf Hall* by Hilary Mantel. She read for a little over half an hour before turning out the light.

Tulia's eyes grew accustomed to the dark as she strained to look around her familiar bedroom. It seemed to take on strange and macabre shapes and shadows during the hours of darkness. She sometimes thought she saw a face or some creature slithering away. As a child she believed that there were shadow people who came into houses and stood watching you sleep. Why was the dark so scary? She listened hard for the slightest sound, but save for the odd car in the distance it was silent. There was nothing.

Tulia's eyelids grew heavy as though something were pulling them down. She felt so tired.

She was woken by scurrying, scratching, scrabbling sounds. Her eyes opened wide and she instinctively drew the duvet up around her neck to protect herself.

The sounds had been hushed, gentle almost, but they had most definitely been there. She wasn't imagining them. Her first thought, which she dismissed almost as soon as she had it, was that a slight breeze had blown through the tiles and into the roof space, but it was a still night with few if any air currents. Her next thought was much more probable, but far more distressing. It could be an animal of some kind. As that thought passed through her mind the noises repeated themselves, this time accompanied by a gentle creaking sound which made her rigid with fear.

'For Christ's sake, get a bloody grip won't you.'

She said this aloud in a whisper that was almost as if someone else was saying it. She wouldn't let it faze or torment her...there had to be a logical, reasonable explanation. 'You'll see,' she said to herself. She needed to busy her mind... distract herself as she waited for the next sounds. What could it be?

She lay there, considering what could be making the sounds. A bat, maybe more than one or because of the scratching sounds a mouse or a rat. Or again, maybe more than one. Perhaps they were nesting up there, perhaps there were babies, or nests of babies! Thoughts of eggs and babies led onto the raft of eggs in *Alien* and *Aliens*, which she had watched with Ralphe, when they were still together, two months ago at least. 'Calm down, calm down you numpty, you're working yourself up for no reason,' the voice in her head whispered.

Then she had an idea. If she got up, went to the loo, then had a drink of water, maybe with all the noise and disturbance it would frighten whatever was up there enough to make it go away. Yeah, she'd do that.

Tulia switched on her bedside lamp and got out of bed. With exaggerated heaviness she stomped across the bedroom floor and continued her leaden steps across the hall and into the bathroom. She flushed and then ran the tap for a few moments before filling the mug. She drank half of it before returning to her bedroom. She listened intently as she laid the mug on the table and got back into bed. All was quiet. She lay with the light on for maybe three minutes before switching it off.

After a further ten minutes or so without any further noise from the attic she concluded that her ruse had worked. The little critters, whatever they were, had been frightened into silence. She turned over onto her side and allowed tiredness to overwhelm her, until she fell asleep again.

◊

'What time did it wake you up?'

'About half one I think.'

'Any idea what it was?'

'A small animal of some sort, I think.'

'Hmm. Maybe we need to go in there and take a look.'

'Yeah probably. If we ask Mr. Grayson do you think he would have a look in there?'

Maya looked at Tulia across the kitchen table and smiled in a way that said 'you must be joking.'.

'The landlord? He'd charge us.'

Tulia laughed.

'You're not wrong there. We would have to pay if we called the council in though wouldn't we?'

'Yep, I reckon so. If we called a company in, like Rentokil, there'd be a fee there as well.'

They both mused over the possibilities.

'Hey, do you think Ralphe might take a look for us? If you didn't mind?'

Tulia pulled a face at Maya.

'I can't say I'd welcome seeing him again.

'I know. The point is, are either you or I going to be brave enough to go in there ourselves?'

Tulia rolled her eyes.

'No. What about Mel-Anne?'

'Err no definitely not. She's worse than you or me.'

'Ok. That doesn't leave us much choice does it? I'll give him a call. Or maybe I'll text him so I don't have to talk to him.'

Maya looked at Tulia.

'You're gonna talk to him anyway so why text?'

Tulia let out a deep sigh.

'I suppose, ok I'll give him a call.'

'You don't think he'll mind?'

'No reason he should. I think us finishing came as a bit of a relief to him as well. I think he knew it had run its course.'

'Let's hope he doesn't mind spiders and their webs.'

◊

'I can't see any signs that there's anything in here at all.'

Ralphe emerged from the small attic door behind the boiler, clutching a torch in his left hand.

'You did look properly and not just a quick glance around didn't you?'

Ralphe stared at Tulia.

'How long was I in there for?'

Tulia looked at Ralphe.

'Over ten minutes. I even lifted up the insulation material. There were no signs of rat or mouse shit anywhere. Look, I've got a rash from touching the fibreglass.'

He lifted and turned his right arm so both girls could see the red blotches that dotted his skin along the length of it.

Tulia was still unimpressed.

'You didn't see anything that might be making those noises? No bird shit up there?'

'No there's nothing in there except the insulation material, dust, spiders and cobwebs.'

'Well, thanks for looking anyway Ralphe. Hope it hasn't used up too much of your time. How's living with your dad?'

'No, no it's fine. It's a roof over my head.'

Ralphe turned towards the front door, stopped and turned round and looked at Tulia. He opened his mouth but then thought better of it and turned back. He made his way to the front door, with Maya behind him, to see him on his way.

'Thanks Ralphe,' said Maya as he opened the door and walked out. He didn't turn around.

'You weren't very welcoming Tule, when he was doing us a favour.'

Maya stepped back into the kitchen.

Tulia shrugged.

'I know, but I couldn't help it. As soon as he came in I felt all claustrophobic again, like he was sucking the air out. I felt I couldn't breathe.'

Maya looked at Tulia.

'That's a bit over the top don't you think? You need to get a grip.'

'Yeah it probably is but I really couldn't help it. It's the way he makes me feel.'

'Oh I meant to ask. Did you have cereal for breakfast this morning?'

'No, toast. Why?'

'Because there wasn't much milk left and I was sure it was half full.'

'No, not me. And while we're on the subject of things disappearing, did you scoff that tin of ratatouille?'

Maya frowned.

'No way. I don't like courgettes.'

'Well it's not in the cupboard and I don't remember eating it.'

'Well neither have I so you must have. I did say you were going senile didn't I?'

Both girls looked at each other.

◊

'Tule, Tule are you awake?'

Maya stood in the doorway of Tulia's bedroom with her hand still on the door knob.

'Yeah I've been awake for the past ten minutes. Did it wake you up too?'

'Yeah.'

'It's the same scrabbling, scratchy sounds I heard the night you were at Mel-Anne's. Whatever Ralphe might say there is something in there.'

The grating, shuffling sounds continued.

'What time is it?'

'Almost three.'

'I need the loo. I'll go and see if that works again to scare the little fucker away.'

Tulia pulled back the duvet and went to the toilet. Maya listened from the doorway with singular attention. As soon as Tulia flushed, the noises ceased. Tulia came back to her room.

'They stopped as soon as you flushed.'

'There has to be something in there. We can't let this carry on. I'll get Ralphe to look again. He must have missed something.'

'I didn't think you'd want him around again?'

'We need to be able to sleep it's as simple as that. I can put up with Ralphe's presence again for a few minutes if we can get to the bottom of this.'

Tulia returned to her room. There were no more sounds from the attic. Maya called out to her.

'I hope you've disturbed it. Try and get some shut eye.'

'I'll call Ralphe in the morning.'

◊

'Have you got a loo roll in your bedroom Tule?'

Tulia walked from the lounge and joined Maya in the toilet.

'No why?'

'Because I know there were three there this morning and now there's only two.'

'You know, when I went to the cupboard before dinner I'm sure some of the tins were in different places to how I remembered them.'

'I know what to do, just to check.'

Maya pulled out a hair from her head and yanked it out, holding its length of about nine inches between her thumb and index finger. She repeated the action holding each hair in separate hands.

'I remember this from one of those old James Bond films I watched with my parents.'

'What Pierce Brosnan?'

'No, the really old one. Oh what's his name? Connery, Sean Connery.'

'Oh - that old? Which film was it?'

'I can't remember any of the titles.'

'Well, I'm no help. Not my sort of thing.'

Maya stuck both hairs across the cupboard door so it overlapped the frame, one right at the bottom and one at the top.

'I've stuck them high up and low down so they can't be seen so easily. Certainly not at eye level anyway.'

'We'll just have to remember they're there and not move them.'

'We'll remember. We'll check when we come in from work tomorrow, see if they have been disturbed.'

'It's like being a spy. Quite exciting really.'

Maya looked at Tulia.

'It's bloody spooky, that's what it is.'

◊

Tulia arrived home at six twenty to find Maya in the kitchen waiting for her.

'Have a look.'

Tulia walked up to the cupboard door and stood on tiptoe. The hair at the top was still in place. She crouched down and found the one at the bottom intact as well.

Bugger, I was hoping they'd have moved.'

Maya nodded her head.

'Likewise. We seem to be back to square one. Did you speak to Ralphe?'

'Yes, I did and he was fine about popping round. He said maybe there were mice in there and he had just missed them. He said he'd bring some traps and see if we can't catch the little buggers.'

'So how come he didn't find any evidence of them when he checked in there the first time?'

'Oh he probably didn't look closely enough or in the right place.'

'Hmm, ok. You've changed your tune a bit haven't you?'

'You mean towards Ralphe?'

'Yeah.'

'Well he's doing his best and as you said he is doing us the favour.'

Maya looked at Tulia.

'So shall we keep the sophisticated burglar alarm in place?'

'Yes, why not. Just in case.'

'Right I need to pop out and get some cash. I forgot to stop on the way home from work. I'll only be ten minutes.'

'Okay, see you in a mo.'

◊

'Maya, Maya. I need to call the bank.'

Maya came out of her bedroom and into the hall where a pale faced Tulia stood, shaking.

'Why, what's happened? You look as though you've seen a ghost.'

Tulia opened her bag up and took out a small printed statement.

'I've got two hundred and fifty less in there than I should have. Someone's taken money from my account.'

Tulia phoned the bank fraud line and reported the incident. She was very shaken and Maya tried to comfort her, hugging her and whispering that everything would be fine.

They were sitting in the kitchen, Tulia on the verge of tears and Maya trying desperately to provide support and comfort for her friend.

'You have checked your account haven't you?'

Maya nodded.

'Yes, through my phone app. Everything's fine, all accounted for.'

A scraping noise came from the attic, followed by a short, sharp grunt and both girls froze in startled horror. That was no mouse or rat. They looked at each other and Maya put an index finger up to her lips. Tulia nodded and they quietly stood up and left the kitchen.

'What do you fancy for tea?'

Tulia glanced at Maya, horrified that she had spoken so loud, but Maya gesticulated to her indicating that she should respond in like manner and then she caught on to what Maya was playing at and spoke with exaggerated volume.

'Oh I don't know,' she said, 'shall we get a Chinese or Indian delivered?'

'Great idea,' said Maya, then she took her phone and dialled 999.

Maya spoke quietly in response to the initial automated emergency services switchboard, after saying which service she required and the address. She was then put through to the local switchboard and told an operative they had an intruder in their attic and they were very frightened. The operative reassured Maya that the police would be there as soon as she could organise a patrol car.

While Maya was speaking to the police, Tulia, despite her heart hammering in her chest, had her phone out and was pretending to scroll through take-aways while making short, loud statements;

'There's loads of Indian places in town. I'm not sure which one to go for.'

'Or shall we have a Chinese?'

She glanced across at Maya who was talking quietly on her phone before she finished.

'They're on their way,' she whispered.

'I fancy an Indian, that alright with you?' Maya said normally.

'Fine,' replied Tulia, whose nerves were once again on edge, now that they weren't doing anything to distract them.

They put the TV on loud and had whispered conversations for most of the time they were waiting. Eventually, after half an hour, there was a knock at the door and two uniformed officers stood on the doorstep.

'I'm Constable Haye and this is Constable Endean, may we come in?'

Constable Haye first questioned the girls and then Constable Endean took statements from them both.

'Your bank will look into the money disappearing from your account Ms Braithwaite. Now if we could just have a look around the house?'

Constable Haye who seemed to be the superior of the two constables, looked through the house quickly before ending up in the kitchen in front of the boiler.

'So you have heard noises from here for some time?' Haye, the female officer squeezed between the back of the boiler and the attic hatchway.

'Yes,' said Maya, 'but the ones we heard just now were definitely not made by an animal. Someone is in there.'

Constable Haye had already switched on a torch before she entered and Endean followed her lead into the dark opening. As they both disappeared into the darkness the girls could see the torch beam dancing in the black. The girls heard muffled voices before Haye emerged and flipped a switch in the attic so that it lit up. She stepped out and was followed seconds later by Endean who was escorting a very dishevelled Ralphe before him.

Both girls gasped.

'Do you know this person?' Constable Haye asked.

'He's my ex-boyfriend. His name's Ralphe Carpenter.'

'You may like to take a look.'

The officer squatted down and re-entered the attic with Maya and Tulia close behind. The whole of the attic was brightly lit now. Endean held onto Ralphe, who stood with his head down, resigned.

'The bulb had been removed but we found it amongst the insulation and put it back. Take a close look and see if anything is familiar.'

Both girls stood to their full height, their eyes widening as the interior was revealed.

In amongst the pale orange insulation material, the TV aerial and wiring were a multitude of carrier bags, food wrappings, cartons and opened tin cans. One of them was an empty can of ratatouille. A make-shift bed with a blanket and cushion was off to one side of the room. An old female doll lay on the cushion. A large plastic bag contained some clothes and when Haye opened the bag and took out the items one by one Tulia gasped.

'They're all Ralphe's. The doll is mine, god this is awful.'

'That's my cushion,' said Maya, 'I hadn't even realised it was missing.

Both girls gazed at each other in horror.

Constable Haye brought out a mobile phone.

'We found this as well.'

As the officer brought the phone up to eye level both girls could see the image used as a background. It was a picture of Tulia with a few clothes on.

'I feel sick, said Tulia.

'There may be others,' said Haye.

'How long could he have been living in here?'

Tulia looked at Maya.

'Could this person have obtained your bank details Ms Braithwaite?'

104

Tulia looked at Maya and the officers looked at the girls in turn. Both girls blanched white.

The End

Shoot From The Hip

'It's very simple Stella, I don't like him.'

Stella Thomas looked hard at her mother, Rita.

'You never like any of my boyfriends.'

'That's because there's always something wrong with them. They're just not for you.'

Stella took a long deep sigh.

'I'm only thinking of you Stella. I don't want you to get hurt.'

'But I do get hurt Mother and it's always because you make me end it.'

Rita smiled.

'Because I care Stella, because I care.'

Rita glanced over towards her husband Brian who was sitting in his chair, trying to be invisible and to appear engrossed in his newspaper. He failed on both counts.

'I'm right, aren't I Brian?'

The broadsheet was lowered revealing the hunched up figure of Stella's father.

'I daresay you are Rita, although... if this bloke is as unsuitable as you say, won't Stella find that out for herself in due course?'

Rita's lips pursed. Her eyes seemed to retreat further into her head.

'It will be too late by then. Stella must act now to stop this...man from taking advantage of her.'

She continued to glare in Brian's direction but he had disappeared behind the paper again.

While her mother's attention was diverted elsewhere Stella rolled her eyes in reaction to her father's pathetic attempt at ploughing the middle ground. He had never, ever stood with her against her mother, siding instead with Rita or, as he had just now, finding some middle ground compromise that angered and frustrated both her and her mother. This was as close as her father ever got to developing a backbone and she knew it would never change, not now. Most of the time he turned a blind eye, leaving Stella at her mother's mercy. But then, in all fairness she never helped herself either with her own subservient attitude. This time, however, she felt more confident. She wouldn't take her mother's abuse lying down.

'How does Duncan take advantage of me? I've only gone out with him twice and you've met him once. How can you know anything about him?'

Rita's eyes narrowed.

'I only needed to meet him once to suss him out. If you know how and where to look it's obvious. But you're so involved you can't see the wood for the trees.'

Stella felt her heart pounding in her chest as her mother revealed, not for the first time, her amazing powers of detecting an 'unworthy '. This was the tag she applied to every bloke she attempted to have some sort of relationship with , not that there had been many.

'I just know it Stella he's no good for you.'

Stella made a noise between a grunt and a cry and nodded. She was beaten already.

'Ok, I'll do something about it.'

Rita beamed.

'At last common sense prevails, doesn't it Brian?'

Brian emitted a sort of bark from behind the paper, which Rita took as confirmation.

'You need to do this now Stella, sooner rather than later. Don't allow him to get his slippers under the bed. When are you seeing him again?'

'Tomorrow night.'

'Well then, first opportunity and all that.'

'Yes mum.'

Stella made her way up the stairs to her bedroom, checking her mobile as she did so. Duncan had sent her another message in the past hour. She waited until she was in her room, with her door closed, before sitting on the edge of her bed and opening it. The message was typical of the type that Duncan sent to her;

> *Thank you for your company last night Stella. I'm sorry I should have thanked you earlier. So looking forward to taking you out on Sunday. Seven o'clock?'*

She smiled as a warm, cosy feeling swept through her. He was such a gentleman. So far he had shown nothing but respect towards her. She would phone him later to confirm the date.

She had bumped into Duncan Fairbrother, literally, at Dawson Manufacturing, the company where she worked. It had been three weeks ago. Duncan had apologised profusely, despite her being the one who had not been looking where she was going, and they had had a brief chat. Duncan was new, it was only his second day, but for whatever reason they seemed to fly into each other's orbit with amazing frequency over the next week or so. It was the Monday morning of his third week when Duncan sidled up to her on their way back from coffee and blurted out an invitation.

'I was wondering whether I could take you out somewhere...this week Stella?'

She must have looked a little startled because Duncan began to back off.

'Of course if you're...'

'No...no I'd love to, thank you for asking.'

Duncan arranged for them to go out for a meal, nothing too elaborate but pleasant enough. He reminded her of herself in many ways. He was a little awkward around people, and reticent about putting his point of view across in case it upset someone else. She could tell he found social gatherings difficult; something she could identify with only too well.

The evening had begun tentatively with both of them on edge, a bit wary. Stella had little experience with men and really had only her father as any form of role model. She had realised, when still very young, that her father was subservient and totally dominated by her mother. She suspected that Duncan had had a similar upbringing which fostered his social awkwardness.

As the food arrived Duncan revealed that he was a vegetarian. This led to the first of many intense yet stimulating discussions between the two of them. Stella had been toying with that way of life after having seen how animals for food were raised and slaughtered but she had not had the courage of her convictions to embrace it. She could hear her mother's voice inside her head;

'Not eating meat anymore? Why ever not? It's not healthy, you'll be ill, you mark my words.'

After that first deeper conversation the tension lifted and they both lightened up and relaxed. It was an enjoyable evening for both of them.

It was a little after ten when Duncan quietly rolled up outside the house and dropped Stella home. Despite there being no twitching of the curtains she knew that her mother would be watching what was going on. Not for the first time Stella thought it was as if her mother had no life of her own except interfering and aligning herself with her daughter's. Sure, she ruled her father with a rod of iron but most of the time he didn't seem to care. She had had these thoughts before, especially when she started seeing a chap she liked. She found her mother's destructive and negative attitude quite sad and pathetic, but she always kept those thoughts to herself.

'See you tomorrow at work Stella. Thank you for a lovely evening.'

She in turn had thanked Duncan and, as he pulled away from the house she had skipped out of his car and up to the front door. As she reached the threshold the door miraculously opened as though it were enchanted. Her father stood to the right, mostly hidden by the door, his hand on the latch, looking very serious as he always did at these times.

'I hope you had a good time Stella,' he whispered, 'prepare for the Inquisition.'

There was no mirth or teasing behind his words and she knew there wouldn't be. He had probably been getting an earful from her mother all evening. She stood up straight and readied herself for the third degree. She walked into the lounge, followed by her father.

'We went to Gables off the roundabout by McDonalds. We had a three course meal. Duncan is a good talker and a very nice man.'

'Oh they're all good talkers, they can all sell fridges to Eskimos. Did he pay?'

'He offered to but I said we'd go Dutch, it was only fair.'

'Hmm. In my day a man would always pay, wouldn't he Brian? Never see a woman paying for anything, it just wasn't done.'

Brian was ensconced behind his paper yet again and responded with a single grunt which could have meant anything or nothing.

'Times have changed mum. Women go out to work. The man isn't the single bread winner. It's just a different world that's all.'

Rita made a derisory snort. It might be the way of the world, but she wasn't having any of it. The country was going down the drain because of it.

A period of silence followed. Stella took the opportunity to remove her coat. If she could go to hang it up in the hall she might be able to make her escape, relatively unscathed. But she never stood a chance. As she turned she was forestalled.

'I don't like the look of him...this chap.'

'So you can tell what he's like from peering out of the window and seeing him sitting in the car, can you?'

Stella surprised herself with her own vehemence. Even her father's paper rustled with the shock. She had never voiced a defence against her mother so strongly before. Her mother eyed her warily.

'What's got into you, getting all aggressive and defensive, eh Stella? It's nothing personal against this chap but...you'll learn as you get older. You read people easier, see things that when you're less experienced in the ways of the world can leave you open and vulnerable.'

'Duncan isn't like that at all. He was very kind, considerate and we got on very well.'

Rita smiled.

'I bet you did. They all behave themselves at the start. They create a good impression so you're taken in and then gradually the layers peel off and the real them is exposed, when it's too late. If they show their true colours from the off it wouldn't ever get started.'

Stella had experienced this form of intrusion before but this time she was determined to speak up for Duncan. Thoughts and words were welling up inside her head and she really wanted to defend him and her right to go out with him. This worried her. It felt as if she might not be able to control it and she would blurt out something...and god knew where that could lead.

'I'm going to bed. It's nearly half ten and I'm up for work in the morning. Night dad, mum.'

Without waiting for a response she turned and walked out of the lounge, hung up her coat and made her way up the stairs. She heard a mumbled 'goodnight Stella' from her father but nothing from her mother. Rita was probably in shock at Stella's standing up to her and then her dismissive attitude. What was the matter with her? She had never walked away from her mother like that before. There'd be hell to pay later.

◉

'Mrs Thomas it's lovely to meet you. I'm Duncan...Duncan Fairbrother.'

Stella beamed. Duncan was brave and a little defiant. She could tell that inside he was writhing and squirming like a ball of snakes. Reluctantly, Rita took Duncan's proffered hand and shook it limply once before releasing it, as though to remain in contact with him would prove fatal. She was grimacing rather than smiling as if this was all so unpleasant she could hardly bear it.

'Mr Thomas, lovely to meet you too Sir.'

Brian was already standing and took a couple of steps to accept Duncan's hand in a firm grasp. Rita said not a word, although her eyes spoke volumes.

'Nice to meet you my boy. Now, where are you proposing to take my daughter tonight?'

Duncan turned and smiled warmly at Stella, who reciprocated.

'We thought we'd take a drive in the country. I know a small traditional public house where we can sit outside in a lovely garden and have a chat.'

Brian looked as though he were going to cry with happiness, until he caught Rita's eye boring into his own.

'Have a good time.'

Stella reached for her coat and handbag.

'We will dad, thank you.'

'You're not one of these who drinks and drives are you?'

Rita's voice sounded like a series of barks. A mischievous grin spread across Duncan's face.

'Yes I do Mrs Thomas, I'm sorry to say.'

He paused for a moment.

'Soda and lime on the rocks.'

Brian and Stella smiled, while Rita glared at Duncan whose comment, she felt, was in very poor taste and not the least bit amusing.

'I meant alcohol.'

Duncan caught her eye.

'I know. But don't worry Mrs Thomas, I don't drink alcohol, don't like the taste.'

Stella turned and made for the hall, Duncan following.

'Don't forget what you promised Stella.'

Stella appeared not to hear as she and Duncan opened the front door.

'Don't wait up,' was her reply.

◎

'You were going to finish with him Stella!'

'No, you wanted me to finish with him mother, it's very different. Duncan is a sweet, sensitive chap and last night was so lovely...'

'I don't care if he's a divine angel, he's up to no good I can tell.'

Stella looked at her mother, wondering why on earth she always saw Stella's world through negative eyes and that men especially were always on the make. Maybe some of them were but most of them weren't.

They were alone in the kitchen. Brian had beaten a tactical retreat, disappearing into the garden on some mumbled pretext.

She didn't want to disobey her mother but there was something about Duncan that attracted her strongly to a relationship with him, made her want to look after and protect him, from her mother for a start. She could feel her resolve hardening, which was another first.

'No mother, he is not. Duncan is a caring, trustworthy soul who hasn't got a bad bone in his body. He likes me and I like him and I know that we are good for each other.'

Rita eye balled her daughter with ill concealed hostility. Stella had never reacted to her like this before, all confrontational and independent. It leant even more urgency to the need to break this relationship before it got further ingrained.

'Well...if you won't listen to reason there is no alternative is there? You can't live at home with your father and me if you insist on still seeing that man!'

Rita folded her arms across her chest as a challenge, a declaration for hostilities to commence.

'You would do that...to get your own way against the wishes and happiness of your only child? What harm does Duncan and I being together do you?'

'You don't know him. He's trouble. But if you know best and want to ruin your life you go ahead...but on your own and under your own roof.'

Stella stood up very erect, taller than her mother and looked her straight in the eye.

'Right OK. It's about time I stood on my own two feet. I'll go as soon as I can find somewhere suitable. It shouldn't take more than a week or two.'

'Stella, you ungrateful brat, how can you treat me in this callous way after everything I have done for you?'

Stella looked at her mother as though seeing her for the very first time. She saw a woman who appeared frail, vulnerable, needy, everything she had supposed her mother never to have been, but she was. She could see it now. Her mother had led an empty, vacuous life, filled totally by herself. But she periodically sustained her meagre existence by feeding off Stella and her father as well. That was all she had.

'I would never have let my mother down the way you have let me down.'

Her mother's continuing diatribe added to Stella's resolve to get away and lead her own life. Her mother's words couldn't hurt her anymore.

'I'm forty six for god's sake mother. It's time I had a life of my own free of your constant interfering and manipulation. I'll be gone as soon as I can.'

Stella turned her back on her mother and walked towards the stairs.

Stella lay on her bed and put her hands behind her head. A fierce determination had welled up inside her and for the first time in her life she was prepared to stand up for what she wanted and what, and who, she believed in. Duncan was a lovely man and she knew they would be very happy together. And maybe, in time, that might mean living together. She smiled at thoughts of Duncan. She felt an overwhelming desire to hear his voice. She would give him a call, just to talk to him. Now, where had she left her phone? Downstairs she thought. She'd go down later and get it.

◙

'I've phoned him so many times since last night. I've left voicemails and texts since yesterday when he didn't show up for work. I'm worried sick.'

'Never you mind pet, he'll turn up, mark my words and there'll be a logical explanation.'

Stella smiled at her father.

'Thanks dad, you're just the support I need. I hope you'll be alright when I go.'

'I've survived fifty years. A few more won't hurt.'

Rita walked in and wrinkled her nose in distaste.

'He's got another woman, that's what it is. Got another woman and run off like the coward he is. See? I told you he was up to no good but you know best. You just didn't listen, did you?'

Stella turned towards her mother, her determination hardening further.

'You're not helping.'

'And you're not helping yourself Stella Thomas. You live in this dream-like fantasy world of yours. You need to get back to reality my girl and be quick about it.'

'Duncan is nothing like the way you portray him, I know. He's a fragile, delicate soul far too unsure of himself to do anything so unpleasant.'

'Says you! What do you know? Where is he? You don't know! You're kidding yourself Stella. In this short space of time you've built up this chap and it's taken you over, so that in your eyes he can do no wrong.'

'Because he hasn't done anything wrong!'

'Yet.'

Why was it that her mother always felt the need to have the last word?

Stella turned her head and glanced at the digital clock beside her. It was six twenty three. Why did she have to be awake so early on a Saturday? Then she thought of Duncan.

She sat up immediately and reached for her mobile. Nothing, he hadn't replied to any of her promptings. What had happened? Where was he? She couldn't believe it was anything to do with her...unless he had done something and couldn't bear to face her at work? For god's sake...no, she was sounding like her mother. Duncan was a decent, if rather apprehensive chap, she had no doubts about that.

She had taken an age to get off to sleep with all the doubts and fears about Duncan swirling around her head. But eventually the working week and her worry caught up with her and she had slowly succumbed. But early or not she was now wide awake and there was no hope of her going back to sleep. She might as well get up. She cleaned her teeth after breakfast before deciding to go for a walk. She didn't return until a little after eight thirty.

Within five minutes of her return there was a loud knock on the front door. Her father went, as he always did and called for Stella to come urgently. He returned to the lounge as his daughter came to the door. Her pace slowed as she came face to face with two uniformed police officers. She invited them in and they followed her into the lounge where both Rita and Brian were now sitting.

'I'm sorry to disturb you all so early on a Saturday morning. I'm Sergeant Crosse and my colleague is Constable Jeffries. There have been some developments in the search for Mr Duncan Fairbrother.'

Stella gasped. What had happened? Something bad – she could feel herself starting to shake. Both officers remained standing as Stella slumped onto the sofa.

'I regret to inform you Ms Thomas that we have found a body. We believe it to be Mr Fairbrother,' said Sergeant Crosse.

Stella burst into tears, heaving uncontrollably. Her father stood up and passed a handkerchief to her and she wiped her eyes. He left his hand momentarily on her shoulder before sitting himself back down in the chair.

Sergeant Crosse continued, as Constable Jeffries stood slightly behind him.

'He was found in Stokesly Wood just a few miles out. I am sorry to say that it appears Mr Fairbrother took his own life, although enquiries are on-going.'

Stella continued to cry, dabbing her eyes.

'I am sorry to have to ask you questions as such a sensitive time Ms Thomas but we have to follow due process. Is that alright?'

Stella nodded and made a croaky 'yes'.

'Are we correct in assuming that a relationship between yourself and Mr Fairbrother had developed, out of work, that is?'

Before Stella could gather herself to reply, she heard a quiet, derisory snort come from her mother. That was enough of a stimulus to get herself together, although she still sniffed and dabbed her eyes with the handkerchief as she replied.

'Yes...he started at Dawson's just over a month ago. We have been out together three times in the last week and a half or so.'

'When you saw him at work or out socially how did he appear to you? Was he upset about anything or with anyone? Was he enjoying his new job? How were things between you and Mr Fairbrother?'

'He was fine, no, better than that. We both were, I thought. I'm sure there was nothing that had upset him. He always seemed happy and full of life. He was kind and considerate and we got along very well. I can't understand why he would take...'

Stella began crying again and wiped her eyes with the handkerchief.

'Thank you Ms Thomas, we appreciate that this is very hard for you at this time. The reason we asked about Mr Fairbrother's state of mind and how things were with the two of you was because he left a note...well a letter really...for you.'

'For me?'

Stella snivelled, then blew her nose.

The other officer reached into a top pocket and drew an envelope out.

'Our apologies, but under the circumstances the letter has been opened and its contents recorded.'

The officer handled the slightly crumpled envelope to Stella who dropped her handkerchief onto her lap as she took it with shaking hands. She could see that it had *Stella* written neatly across the middle in Duncan's elegant, although rather small script.

She removed a single piece of lined A4 paper which was folded three times and opened it. She scanned it quickly noting it was very long before beginning to read.

My darling Stella

You clearly cannot know or comprehend the magical impact meeting you has had on me. To merely see you every day would have been sufficient to brighten my mood and outlook, but to have you accept my invitation to go out was like manna from heaven for me. I am not being melodramatic or over the top when I tell you that I was transformed by your company such that my view of life had changed completely.

I dared to think that you might feel something similar. Or at least there would be a hope that over a period of time you might think of me in that way.

I am a simple man but due to my shyness and insecurities have always run away from everything that a life had to offer especially if it meant dealing with other people. That was the case until I met you.

I have torn my head apart trying to work out why you ended it. I cannot understand what it was that I had done wrong that has made you walk away from something that had only just started to be built. I am not...

Stella raised her head from the letter and looked at the officers, her eyebrows furrowed, her mouth slightly open.

'I didn't...'

'Perhaps if you finish reading the letter in its entirety before making any comments Ms Thomas?'

Sergeant Crosse's tone was soft.

'Yes, yes of course.'

Her eyes returned to the page.

I am not concerned with how you finished with me Stella. I understand, maybe hope that it was too painful or too unpleasant for you to do it face to face. I refuse to believe that it was because you were too timid, too much of a coward to tell me to my face. In such a short space of time I believe I have come to know you better than that.

Stella let out a cry and dabbed her eyes again.

I, though, am a coward. Having met you, spent time with you I cannot be without you. For decades I have hidden myself away, looked in another direction or simply run away from any sort of connection or intimacy with another. I couldn't bear the thought of it and then you floated into my life.

You gave me so much; purpose; stability and a lust for life that I had never thought possible. Without you I return to the empty vacuous being I have always been. I am sorry for my weakness and I beg you to forgive me but I cannot live in this greedy, loveless world without the one person who changed my world beyond recognition. I hope you can find happiness with someone.

Always yours

In love

Duncan

Stella's eyes watered again as she clutched Duncan's letter to her chest, sobbing and heaving in equal measure.

'Ms Thomas, once again I apologise for having to...'

'I didn't finish with him, nothing could have been further from my mind. Duncan was right. I DID feel exactly the same way about him as he clearly did for me. It's so strange. What is going on here?'

'Well, that is what we are trying to establish. The letter was found in Mr Fairbrother's left trouser pocket. His mobile phone was found in his right and it had been left open with the text message from you ending the relationship.'

Stella creased her brow again and her breathing and heartbeat began to increase.

'What did it say?'

Constable Jeffries pulled out her notebook and flicked through some pages before coming to a halt.

'The message was received at six fifty two on Thursday just gone. It says,

Can't see you anymore

you're not right for me

Stella frowned so hard her eyebrows almost met in the middle.

'I didn't send that message.'

'It was sent from your phone on that date and at that time Ms Thomas, with your number at the top of the message.'

'I'm telling you I did not send that message.'

The two officers exchanged a glance.

'Well in that case can you explain,'

Brian had never seen his daughter move so fast.

The End

Hear✝Land

Present day

Erin Kyra's great-grandfather, Joshua Stable lay gasping his last breaths in the massive mahogany bed. As she stood, thinking about the decision she would soon have to make, she fixed her gaze on the heavy headboard, and the intricate carvings of symbols and incantations that covered its surface. The ailing man was layered in heavy covers, despite the heat in the plush decorated room. Above Erin's head a chandelier sparkled and twinkled in the natural light that shone through the coloured glass of two large arched windows.

It was a sumptuous room, which like the rest of the mansion, had changed little since Joshua was born there in 1868.

Erin glanced around the room at the two mahogany sideboards that complimented each other on opposite walls, while the ornate wardrobe stood proudly to attention like a guarding sentinel. There used to be two but after Joshua's wife, Violet Dakota Pryce died in 1966 at the age of ninety five, one had mysteriously disappeared.

Erin caught a movement out of the corner of her eye.

Joshua addressed the family gathered around his bed, his voice still strong, but with a less forceful tone.

'After my coffin is lowered, the lid must remain open.'

He coughed and gasped with the effort of speech as his final breaths of mortal life ebbed away. He laid his head back on the pillow, a filmy glaze passing across his once bright, cobalt eyes like a translucent curtain drawn across a stage. He coughed again, rasping and wheezing. Erin and the rest of the family moved in closer to hear the dying man's last words

'Listen to me, I only have moments. You must pinion my shoulders, ankles and neck with metal spikes and then drive a blackened hawthorn stake through my heart. Make sure they all penetrate the floor of the coffin and anchor me in the earth below.'

He choked and cleared his throat again, blood mingling with his saliva. His face, once strong and determined, was now ravaged by the demands, both physical and spiritual, of the extended lifespan that he had never sought, but that had been bequeathed to him. His skin was taut, stretched like parchment over the protruding bones of his face. He lay with his eyes staring open.

Erin asked in a small voice, 'Has he gone?'

Erin was the youngest member of the family. She had broken up from school only two days earlier for the summer.

'No, I haven't,' Joshua rasped, chuckling a little.

Erin jumped, her short cropped blonde hair bouncing on her head. Her hair style lent her an androgynous appearance. She was wearing a pink lace ruffle crop top and a pair of white, three quarter length trousers. She wore nothing on her feet, having taken her pink canvas pumps off when she arrived with her mother and father, Amy and Angus Gordon and her older brother Jay.

'I'm sorry great-grandfather, it's just that for a moment you looked so...still and serene. I thought you had...'

Joshua turned his head slowly to the left and Erin felt the intensity of his gaze upon her.

'If I appear so tranquil it is because I leave you in the hope that on my quietus I know you will all come together and make the right decision for our disparate kindred to maintain and endure.'

Erin opened her mouth to reply but before she could speak there came a gurgling and then a rattling from Joshua's throat before silence fell like a weight in the room. A dark shadow fell upon his constricted facial features followed by a tranquillity that was in marked contrast to the way Joshua Stable had lived his life.

'The last hunter of his generation,' said Josephine Rebecca Smythe. One hundred and twenty three years old, she was Erin's great aunt, dressed sombrely in a dark grey patterned blouse and black skirt. Despite her years she stood tall and upright.

'The end of an era in one sense then,' said Robyn, her daughter. At eighty years old, she looked little over half that age. She was shorter than her mother but still taller than Berkley Rossiter, her husband.

Robyn's son, Harold turned to look at Erin. 'And maybe the start of another,' he said. Erin felt the eyes of the whole family on her as they stood around Joshua's bed.

'Or maybe the end,' said Josephine, a small smile creasing her lips.

Nine pairs of eyes looked on Erin, five of them with a relieved 'at-last' countenance and the rest in shocked surprise.

'You mean to terminate our family heritage!' Erin's elder brother Jay was incensed. Jay was twenty one and had developed some of the personality traits of his uncle, Davis John Smythe.

'Come Jay, it is our way and always has been. Following the death of the patriarch or matriarch hunter the remaining family cast their vote as to whether to continue the family 'tradition'. As Joshua is at liberty to cast his final vote, despite his passing, we are locked at five against and five for. Erin, the youngest, has the final vote. That is where your preference lies does it not, my child?'

Erin glanced at Josephine, who she knew saw things the way she did before looking at her mother, Amy, then at each of her family in turn. She could feel her confidence in her authority rising. She had reached her conclusion.

'Yes...yes it is.,' she said. 'We have sacrificed too many family members and for what? A cause that few mortals understand and now no longer believe in. It is time for them to accept the burden. We in this family have done our bit over the aeons. It is time for the other hunting clans to step up to the plate if they so desire.'

'Well said,' said Josephine.

Harold spoke. 'So that's it then? Our family legacy formed over two centuries through six generations of sanguisuge hunters, extinguished by a stripling of a girl with only, what, two minor hunts to her name.'

At forty five, Harold had been a venator of sanguisuge for almost three decades. He was aware of the conventions and due process, and largely accepted them, but he wasn't prepared to let all that they had achieved be washed away without marking the occasion with some form of stand. He wore clothing that was simple and functional; a dark patterned camouflage shirt, mainly greens and dark grey, black combat trousers with multiple pockets and a long black trench coat with many inner pockets within the lining.

'I believe you're missing the point here old son.'

Angus Guscott Gordon, husband to Amy and father to Jay and Erin, turned his gaze on Harold. He was a short man, barely five foot five, but it would be a mistake to underestimate him based on his stature. He looked after the family fortune and investments. They all had their function.

'In what way?' Harold asked forcefully.

Angus smiled benevolently.

'Although I am what you term an 'interloper' in your family and its heritage Harold, those of us who have joined the fold fully take on and become one with the family inheritance, as we all should and must.'

The other faces were all fixed on him.

'Josephine has experienced the greatest loss, as we all are well aware, and certainly over a longer time span. I believe in what the family has done, keeping mortals safe from an enemy of which most are ignorant. But now with Joshua's passing a closure of sorts has occurred and a new dawn has arisen. This vote was put in place to allow for a pause, a reflection to take a closer look at ourselves, what we do and how we do it.'

Harold made to interrupt but Angus held out his hand to forestall him.

'I know Harold, I know that Amy and I are not, and never have been, at the sharp end. I am aware that there are those in this family who believe that if we do not fully participate, then we should have less of a say in what transpires. But it doesn't, does it? All of us, no matter how much or little we devote to the cause, have a say, because it affects us all. I know that after Hillary's disappearance in 1992, and Louella's thirteen years ago, Amy changed in her stance. What we must remember is that it is the ones left behind who bear the loss, but

130

together, collectively. We must stand together whatever the decision. It is the only way for this family to survive.'

Out of the silence that followed Constance Rossiter sniffed back a few tears before the consoling arm of her husband George, enveloped her shoulders.

'I'm sorry Connie, George or anyone else if I have opened old wounds but these truths need to be aired. If we cannot discuss this like mature adults then what hope is there?'

Constance Rossiter habitually wore black ever since the disappearance of their daughter thirteen years previously. Her husband George refused to be so morbid, as he termed it, but supported his wife in her stance. If that was the way she felt, then that was good enough for him. For all of them though, closure remained an issue.

A considered silence followed as each person in the bedroom was filled with their own turmoils and troubles, some historic, some more recent. Erin was fully aware that the loss of family members was a constant darkness. For some though, it provided the spur to continue. What would her decision mean for them all? She knew that whatever her decision was it would be accepted over time. For some it would be hard to give up a lifestyle and duty that very few had the skills to achieve and maintain. If that meant a cessation of searching for their loved ones then there may be some - Harold and Jay sprung into her head - prepared to go it alone. And they would argue, what else would they do?

Robyn looked at her mother Josephine who gave the slightest nod in response. Robyn bent down towards Joshua's constricted death-mask face. With reverence she opened the mouth and retracted the upper lip. The teeth of his maxilla were in extraordinary condition for a human being over a century and a half old. The family members strained forward to gain a better view of the proceedings.

'There is no evidence of lengthening canines,' said Robyn as if there could have been any doubt. She replaced the upper lip manually, as the elasticity of Joshua's skin was becoming constricted in death.

Erin looked down on her great-grandfather, the legacy that he had brought about preying on her mind. Both she and Jay, being the two youngest had been prepared by the family since the beginning of their teenage years. Ultimately though, the choice was theirs, and theirs alone.

Jay had helped her from when she had turned thirteen, the age when family history and expectations had begun to be related to her. She had known from an early age that her family, including herself, were different from her peers. That said, she had never allowed that difference to be used against her. She was popular at school, if a trifle over-confident at times, which occasionally bordered on arrogance. She remembered Jay reassuring that she should be herself, but not at the expense of dismissing others who didn't share the gift that their family possessed.

There had only been the one confrontation when she was close to turning fifteen. She remained proud of how she had handled herself then. The easiest option would have been to use her physical strength and prowess to overpower her assailant, an older girl, Regina Murdoch. Gina, as she was known, had taken a dislike to this precocious upstart who was a year below her. She had wanted to teach her a lesson she wouldn't forget.

Erin had remained calm and unassuming and slowly had won Regina over, convincing her that she wasn't at all the way Regina portrayed her.

Before she had turned thirteen she had been a little aloof and stand- offish, but as Jay had tried to explain to her at the time, that was just her trying to discover who she was.

132

She was faced with a similar crisis now. She didn't want any more of her family to die or go missing. What they did was dangerous and probably unappreciated by humans. And yet, there was the history of what this family meant. She wanted to be a part of that and make a difference. She wanted to follow in the footsteps of Aunt Hillary and cousin Louella in the female line of hunters. But not if it meant losing any more family. She looked around at them all with a warm feeling of belonging.

'We still follow Joshua's request to the letter,' she said.' All of us, whether we have sanguisuge blood flowing in our veins or not, must abide by these strictures at the time of our own passing.'

All murmured their agreement.

It had been early evening when they all gathered, at Joshua's behest, to his bedside. The light was failing and the eight lavish wall lights provided a dusky atmosphere. Both windows were slightly open. Joshua always believed in fresh air.

Now as she stood with the others, Erin's head was full of the family history Harold had told her a mere six months ago, in preparation for this day. She starred at the corpse on the bed and felt a wave of remorse as she remembered the tragic incident that had formed the roots of the family.

Joshua's grandfather Sir Peregrine Stable was the first of the family to hunt vampires, when he and his wife, Tryphena Rider lost their first child, a babe of less than a year, to a young female vampire. The year was 1827 and Sir Peregrine was already a formidable statesman who had accumulated considerable wealth and influence during the reign of George III. After the murder of their child, he began hunting vampires, quietly and without fuss, despatching them without mercy.

But it was Raynor, Peregrine's youngest child and only son who would really embrace the sanguisuge cause. He it was who began to write down his, and later Joshua's, experiences of that murky world betwixt and between. It was also he who saw to the family's financial security, which lasted to the present day.

Raynor Stable died from natural causes in 1897 when Joshua was twenty nine. By that time Joshua was on his way to becoming an effective and worthy sanguisuge adversary, despite an inauspicious beginning when in 1881 he was attacked and bitten by a sanguisuge. The beast, for such it was, being a quadruped rather than a bipedal human, was injured and frightened off by Raynor. Despite his wounds Joshua made a full recovery and was taught many valuable lessons which he never forgot.

His destiny as a hunter was assisted considerably when three years later at the age of sixteen Joshua accompanied Raynor during a mass hunt which purportedly featured perhaps thirty to forty vampire hunters and slayers of all types and persuasions. This was deemed auspicious because of a rumoured large vampire gathering. It was too good an opportunity to miss.

Raynor had continued the writing of sanguisuge and hunter history and this incorporated tales and experiences of blood suckers from around the globe. Repeatedly he emphasized that not all vampires were the evil, parasitical monsters portrayed in many legends. There were some civilised, refined and good ones to be found as well, ones that never fed on human blood. His lesson for Joshua was simple; never judge a vampire by its canines but by how it behaves.

The collection of hunters began to fan out, enacting their plan of surrounding the vampire enclave by closing off as many escape routes as they could. But Joshua was uneasy.

He confided his growing foreboding to Raynor, who had learnt to listen to his son's perhaps superior senses. Joshua had perceived that all was not as it appeared.

'There's something not right about this.'

He detected that a small group of hunters were further on edge – more so than would be normal. They seemed to be focussed on a specific single target. From Raynor's wisdom on past experiences, Joshua anticipated that they would soon reveal themselves and their motives. Raynor quietly advised Joshua to have his wits about him and be on his guard;

'Stay alert and we'll be fine. There's something amiss here boy, as you say, and we're right in the thick of it.'

As the circle of hunters and slayers moved slowly forward encircling and ensnaring their quarry, which could number up to one hundred, Joshua was amazed at the variety of what passed for vampires across the globe. Some were human derived, but others, despite being bipedal, bore scant resemblance to humans. Others were clearly more closely aligned with the beasts and creatures of the wild. As they armed and primed their weapons they were disturbed by a large shape gliding above them. Looking up, Joshua saw an air borne vampiric creature for the first time. The beast was acting as a sentinel and as the hunters were spotted their presence and location was revealed to all.

The vampires scattered in all directions, sowing confusion in numbers to bewilder the enemy – a few took to the wing; others metamorphosed into a wolf or a bat; others formed trailing mist and evaporated; while others that were feral beasts, some very large, defended themselves against their human adversary.

Joshua kept close to Raynor who in turn was keeping very close to the group of four hunters who appeared to have ulterior motives. Joshua allowed himself periodic glances around the battlefield. He witnessed the flying creatures being immobilized with hardened hawthorne crossbow bolts, and hunters being devoured by vampiric creatures with monstrous jaws. Some of the beasts even Raynor had not seen before.

The group of four in front of them ignored all other quarry; they were stalking a female sanguisuge who was giving a good account of herself as a warrior, disarming and incapacitating any hunter or slayer she encountered, but not killing them.

As the four approached this lithe, athletic creature she espied Raynor and Joshua behind her four adversaries. She addressed both Raynor and Joshua calmly and with dignity.

'I am Dania of the House of Javier and I request your aid. I have no wish to kill, even those who wish me vanquished. These four have been recruited by other vampires, for no other reason than to eliminate those sanguisuge with a conscience and empathy towards mortals, so leaving only those uncivilised, base creatures to prey on humans.'

As the first two hunters engaged Dania in combat it was clear to Raynor and Joshua that she could neutralize two, maybe three, but if all four were to engage her, despite her physiological prowess and advantages, there was no guarantee she would survive. In addition Raynor had learnt much about Javier's vampiric dynastic lineage, as well as a plethora of other sanguisuge creatures. He could easily believe that there was an internal battle for power and control.

'I speak to the four hunters to desist your attack on this sanguisuge from the House of Dania and request your deployment elsewhere on the battle front.'

Raynor's request was met by the other two hunters turning around and engaging both he and Joshua in battle. They clearly were not looking to only disarm.

Despite his lack of years and physical strength Joshua was lithe, fit and very manoeuvrable. He swiftly incapacitated his adversary making him fall and knock himself out on a protruding rock. Then he moved to help Dania. The hunter he engaged with was enormous, at least six feet eight, so Joshua stayed low, forcing the human beast to bend in an effort to catch him a blow. But this was hard work and Joshua began to tire. He stood upright, allowing the giant to connect with more blows, while failing to muster any force behind his own. But the goliath too was beginning to feel the effects of the exertion and he too began to slow down. Joshua took note of this and gained confidence, renewing his attack with increased vigour. But in his haste he had become careless, realising too late that the colossus's tiredness was a ruse and he had now left himself open. He narrowly evaded sweeping strikes with two curved blade weapons before being caught with a blow from a foot which launched him into the air and left him sprawling in a semi conscious heap. The giant stood over him gloating in his supposed victory.

'I am Llewellyn Reep, sanguisuge slayer, and you are mine, little boy.'

'Not today, time to sleep.'

Llewellyn swayed a little, buckling at the knees before collapsing flat on his face to reveal the smiling figure of Dania standing behind him. She reached a hand down to the prostrate Joshua and pulled him up to his feet.

'You are brave for one so small.'

'Everyone is small against that tree trunk. What the hell did you do to him?'

Dania smiled and looked over Joshua's shoulder at the approaching figure of Raynor.

'It is refreshing to find a Venator who believes in the word of a sanguisuge, I thank you.'

Raynor made a small obeisance.

'And it is equally refreshing to discover a sanguisuge who speaks the truth and would ask a mortal to believe it. I should say that it was Joshua who first detected your predicament.'

'He has a nose for such things, it is clear.'

Dania sniffed the air and poked the tip of her tongue out before addressing Joshua.

'You have been bitten and allowed yourself to be drawn.'

'Three years ago when I was thirteen, it is of no consequence.'

'I admire your courage but you are in error. What manner of creature was it that attacked you?'

'A beast resembling a gigantic mantis but with a distorted human head.'

'An Aswang. You need to be mindful always of that attack. Was it killed?'

'No,' said Raynor, 'I wounded it but it managed to escape. I do not believe the wound I inflicted was mortal.'

'As long as it continues to walk this earth it will seek you out to finish what it started. It will not be able to escape the taste of your blood on its tongue and that will torment it and drive it to distraction.'

Joshua was not reassured by the revelation.

'May I ask what was the meaning behind the attack you have just experienced?'

The fighting around them had ceased and none of the other hunters appeared to realise, or perhaps they did not care, that there was still a vampire in their midst. Perhaps she posed no threat as she was talking to Raynor and Joshua.

'I will first say that the giant is merely...sedated, I suppose you could call it. He will recover in due course. As to the nature of my predicament...I am not entirely sure.'

Dania eyed the two mortals.

'I would perhaps be more comfortable in revealing my...troubles if I was in possession of your names. Clearly you are father and son...'

Raynor inclined his head, his mane of hair moving as one with his head.

'Forgive me Dania, I meant no slight, if I may address you in such a familiar manner. I am Raynor Stable and this is my son, Joshua.'

Dania smiled, revealing the tips of her canines, which slowly retracted until they disappeared. She turned slightly towards Joshua.

'Now that the giant is...shall we say rendered somewhat shorter, you no longer look so small.'

'Why were they trying to kill you?'

'I am not sure that that was their aim. I think they wanted me alive...well, as alive as an undead can be.'

'To what end?'

'As I calmly explained when I saw you first perhaps I should start further back. You are aware of the thirteen sanguisuge houses founded by Javier?'

Raynor and Joshua exchanged a glance.

'We are. Some date from Roman times while others are more recent, relatively speaking.'

'Yes, I was turned in the year 1200 by your chronology, the twelfth founder. The final founder, Benjamen, followed one hundred and sixty seven years later. With all thirteen houses in place Javier turned his back on us all and permitted us to evolve and develop as we would.

But then of course we, that is, the thirteen houses of Javier, are not the only sanguisuge out there. There are others, as you probably know some former mortals while others are of a more primitive, bestial nature. I believe another group of sanguisuge, possibly of a more base type, although I cannot be sure as I have no evidence, have joined forces with some human sanguisuge hunters to eliminate or capture the more civilised, enlightened vampires for their own ends. What that is I am unable to discern...yet.'

'A civil war of sorts?'

'Yes Joshua, I suppose you could term it like that.'

'And all for power and control?'

'To an extent, Raynor.'

'How so?'

'If the perpetrators are mortal based sanguisuge then I would have some agreement with your assertion. If however they turn out to be from a more brutish primal stock then it may be no more than a group of predators trying to remove another group of predators who feed and survive on the same prey. Some of us have relinquished the drinking of human blood...well...almost.'

'There is good and bad in all. That is one lesson I learnt very early in my hunting evolution.'

'Not everyone is so discerning.'

'So...in these Houses do you have regular meetings or councils that draw up how the future is mapped out, or Elders who lead all the Houses?'

'No... there is no structured hierarchy at all. Each House is free to choose and go their own way at the behest of the founder although that is not always the case.'

A groan from the massive body of Llewellyn reminded them of the battle they had engaged in.

'It has been a pleasure to meet and engage with such an enlightened sanguisuge but I fear it is time to make our departures.'

'Indeed, Raynor Stable. Before we go, in thanks for your assistance and as recompense for your earlier experience with the Aswang, as well as a gift that will stand you in good stead for your future struggles - I would take it as a high honour and privilege if you would accept my offer, a blood gift to you.'

Raynor's surprise was matched only by Joshua's. Raynor spoke first.

'I am humbled by your generous and courageous offer but for myself I would decline. However if you have no objection, Joshua I am sure would be equally proud to receive such a token of your munificence...if HE has no opposition to my proposal?'

Joshua's eyes and mouth opened wide in stupefaction as what was being offered became clear.

Another groan came from the ground to one side.

'I am content to do as you wish,' said Dania. 'There is not the time now, but rest assured I shall see you again Joshua Stable, if that is your wish.'

With that final parting Dania formed into a wispy trail of mist before transforming into a bat and disappearing into the night. Raynor looked at his son.

'Well Joshua, it seems you have a rendezvous to keep. Let's head for home.'

Raynor turned and began walking away. Joshua stood for a moment before turning and glancing at the prone figure of Llewellyn Reep. He approached him and knelt down at his side, placing a honed, blackened hawthorn stake at his neck, the point penetrating some way into the flesh.

'Before I go, I need some information from you please, good sir.'

Llewellyn grunted in response so Joshua pushed the stake deeper.

'I should tell you that I have no compunction about penetrating your jugular vein with this stake, so talk...'

Joshua leant further pressure and the skin around the point went white.

Llewellyn Reep opened his mouth...

Some months later, as the whole family was now aware, Dania made good on her promise and visited Joshua one clear autumnal night. Joshua never revealed how the process was carried out, although he did express his admiration for Dania and some of the other founders of the Houses of Javier who conducted themselves in a civilised manner.

The blood gift bestowed by Dania had passed down the generations, manifesting itself in increased longevity, greater physical strength, endurance and flexibility and an improved immune response both chemical and physical. As far as Joshua or any other member of the family knew, there were no disadvantages to be found as the amount of sanguisuge blood in the circulatory system never amounted to more than five percent of the whole. But it was more than enough to even up the playing field a little.

This history weighed on Erin's mind as she was brought back to the present. None of her friends at school had to make a decision with so much riding on it. It was in one sense, a curse and in another, a privilege and between those two points of view, for her it meant a dilemma.

'So, is that it then with my casting vote? Do we now just bury great-grandfather with those...metal spikes through him and then...then forget about what we used to represent as a family and get on with our lives as though we were normal?'

Erin's tone suggested the unease she felt in her decision.

Jay fixed her with a steely glare, his blue-grey eyes evidence of his defiance. He had embraced the family cause as an honour.

'It would seem so, thanks to you, although I may refuse to...'

They all felt it to a greater or lesser extent. Erin stiffened and looked around at the others. But it was Harold who was the first to react, nodding at Erin and slowly reaching inside his inner coat with his left hand while popping something into his mouth with his right.

Then he extracted a glistening black hawthorn stake from his inner pocket and gripped it tightly.

'We are no longer alone,' he stated although his words were only echoing what everyone else was thinking.

Erin removed a small bottle concealed in an inner pocket and took a sip of holy water before tipping it up onto her index finger and marking the sign of the cross on her forehead.

As one, the others moved to retrieve the weapons concealed within their coats or pockets, even the non hunters among them. There was danger in association.

Ethereal wisps of vapour began to coalesce to one side of the bedroom accompanied by an acrid, coppery taint that left no doubt as to the nature of what was materialising before them. But to what end?

At first the haze collected a little above ground level as though whatever was forming was restricted in height. But as the miasma thickened and merged to form a physical body it became apparent that the figure appeared small, before manifesting in front of them in a position of supplication by kneeling on one knee, head bowed. The transfiguration reached its zenith as the kneeling human figure remained prostrate before them.

'Forgive my intrusion, I mean no disrespect. Accept my presence of my own free will amongst you, a family of Sanguisuge Venators, as testament to the integrity of my coming before you in this manner. I am Dania, from the House of Javier.'

The whole family were poised, clutching their weaponry with which to defend themselves, should that prove necessary, all their senses heightened.

'How have you been able to enter without being invited?'

The rest of the family smiled at Erin's naivety.

'For Joshua to have permitted you entrance is enough Dania, although I would welcome how that came to pass. And please, stand.'

Erin felt no embarrassment at her inexperience. She was keen to learn.

The woman raised herself to her feet and stood surveying the nine faces before her, some more at ease than others. Her eyes eventually came to rest on the prone figure in the bed.

'May I?'

'By all means,' said Josephine.

Dania approached the bed and stood gazing down at the corpse of Joshua Stable.

'He was a principled and noble mortal. Our paths crossed only intermittently but I always found him the same.'

Fascinated, Erin came around to the other side of the bed and observed the sanguisuge. She had not been so close to one before.

Josephine smiled.

'My father spoke well of you too as an honourable and humane being. He also alluded to, but never fully discussed, your being the source of the blood gift bestowed on him and in consequence, on all of us.'

Dania was peering down at Joshua's face, clearly reminiscing.

'The trouble with living so long is that so many memories are available. I am the spring from which that life-sustaining gift flowed, yes. He was only sixteen at the time but with his father Raynor, he helped me survive an attack by four sanguisuge venators who were under the orders of other vampires. He engaged Llewellyn Reep, a brute of a man, in combat and held his own despite his, by comparison, limited experience and stature. It was an extremely brave and gracious gesture.'

Dania observed Erin looking at her and smiled back at her, almost maternally.

'You are too kind,' said Josephine, 'I barely recall Grandfather Raynor. He died when I was three years old.'

Dania looked directly at Erin.

'I should have expected your defences to be enacted. You should always remember, little one, that not every vampire is susceptible to the purity of holy water. Some are beyond its effects.'

She turned from her position and wrinkled her nose, taking a step or two away from Harold who was still chewing.

'Garlic is not as strong a protection as it once was although, as with all protection, it depends on your adversary,' said Dania before looking at Josephine directly.

'As you are all aware, I had offered the blood gift to Raynor in the first instance but he politely refused it. He, though, suggested that Joshua should receive it. I would have been honoured to bequeath it to the both of them, but it was not to be. There has been so much death on both sides, especially in the early days. But fortunately a more evolved enlightened approach has been adopted by some members of the House of Javier and their brethren.'

'So you rarely take human blood?'

Connie spat out the question as though it were painful to hold it in her mouth a moment longer. Dania looked at her and seemed to sense something about her accusatory and unforgiving tone.

'Yes, now. I allow myself the blood of certain types of mortal, I will elaborate no further at this juncture but it is a rare occurrence undertaken to keep my sanguisuge self in relative health. If I may say, I am sorry for the loss that you have endured.'

'You can spare me your sympathetic diatribe. You have been a predator...a parasite like all of your kind and yet you believe that all your previous blood lust can be undone and forgiven by an awakening...a renouncing of the blood. For those of us still counting the days since the loss of loved ones, I can assure you that it does not.'

Dania looked at Connie with sorrow in her eyes.

'I did not seek out this undead existence, although when it was offered to me by Xaverius, as he was then known, I decided, after some deliberation to accede for reasons that now, eight hundred years later, I can barely recall and would find impossible to explain and to agree with.'

Dania turned and glanced at Erin once more.

'I sense the unease and ambiguity within you, child. I will relate something that may be of assistance in your deliberations.'

She cast a glance over all of them and, seeing no refusal, continued.

'I too have had my challenges. The first happened a mere fifteen years after my turning, in what would be, according to your mortal calendar, the year of Magna Carta. I was living quietly and unobtrusively, or so I thought, in a village in England when I was arrested

147

and imprisoned on charges of witchcraft. I would in all probability have perished, being a young and inexperienced sanguisuge, had it not been for my only convert who rode miles to summon help and, for the time, a very understanding vampire hunter who delayed my staking until two of my brethren returned with my convert.'

Dania lowered her head.

'In my shame, I now recount what transpired following my release. It will only confirm in your eyes what you believe all sanguisuge are created for. My two rescuers from the Houses of Sheridan and Lochlan laid the village to waste, slaughtering all before them, men, women and children, all defenceless in the wake of two murderous, monstrous, powerful sanguisuge. Even the vampire hunter who had helped me was not spared when he tried to protect a group of women and children. I was ignorant of my brethren's overwhelming desires, and powerless to prevent the bloodshed and carnage that followed, even if I had known about it before hand. Both of the Houses of which they form the founding path are based on strict adherence to blood lust criteria stemming from their mortal histories. It was following this heinous episode that I renounced all blood, including that of adding to my House, except that which is essential to survival. I still hold my head low at the memory of it all.'

'And so you should.'

There was no forgiveness nor empathy in Connie's tone.

'I offer this to the youngest Stable as a testament of what unseen, unknown fortune destiny may deliver. While you can make a difference I urge you not to give that up without thoughtful consideration.'

Dania looked up at Erin, then Connie and George in turn.

'If I may be permitted to perform one small service that may aid you in your...'

'There is nothing we could want from you,' said Connie.

Neither she nor George had ever been hunters, although their only child had just begun along that path when she had disappeared.

'Your daughter...'

Both Connie and George snapped to attention.

'Louella...' they uttered in unison.

'Louella.'

'You have knowledge of her?'

'I do and I would share it with you as a token of empathy at your continued suffering and torment at the uncertainty of your daughter's providence.'

Immediately the whole family drew closer to Dania, at what would be a pivotal and momentous development. Despite years of searching and asking questions none of the missing family members had left a trace. Their fate was unknown.

'She lives...as a sanguisuge.'

'No!'

George barked out his frustration while Connie's legs buckled under her, unable to bear the weight of this news. In anger she pushed away with force those hands that came to her aid.

'I am fine,' she snapped. Connie's eyes were flaming and defiant.

'You are wrong vampire. She does not live, she is an undead.'

Dania looked confusedly at Connie, then George and then around the faces of all the family.

'You would turn your back on one of your own when there is the potential that she is still your daughter?'

'Louella is still of the Stable family, make no mistake about that,' Josephine boomed out, 'and so are the others who have probably sacrificed their mortal lives for a higher, nobler cause. As you have observed Dania, nerves remain raw in this family. That is why we are on the verge of relinquishing our sanguisuge hunting heritage.'

'I see. I would expect Joshua to have been in favour of continuation, knowing him as I did.'

'And you would be correct. At the time of every passing a plebiscite is enacted either for or against the preservation and continuation of our tradition. As you know, Erin has the casting vote as the ballot, as it stands is equal. Therefore the die is cast.'

Dania paused for a moment and glanced at Erin, before turning back to the others.

'And what of Louella and your other lost brethren? Are they left to their fate, a fate not sought by any of them?'

'You know of Davis and Hillary?'

'Oh so much more do I know than you will ever know. I know of Josephine's brother, D'Arcy and sister in law, Angela, slain in 1948 by their own father, Joshua. I know of sister Maud killed in 1934 by vampires who had aligned themselves with the Nazi party...would you like me to go on?'

Josephine cast her eyes to the floor at the memory of her sister. Her death had been very hard on all of them at the time, especially Joshua.

Erin looked surprised, she was hearing this information for the first time.

'What of Davis, my son? It was so long ago.'

Josephine's voice rattled in her throat.

'Time is relative, Josephine. When he was attacked in 1963 by a horde of sanguisuge Upierczi he was left barely clinging to any form of life, but following on from the attack there is nothing, no firm news of his death or whether he lives as a sanguisuge of sorts.'

'Of sorts? What does that mean?'

'It means he may no longer be recognisable as a former mortal, such are the changes that could have occurred following his mortal death.'

'He is a creature...a beast?'

'He may be. Nothing is known for certain.'

'And Hillary?'

Harold's quest to find his sister was at the heart of him hunting sanguisuge, the task he had dedicated his life to after she vanished in 1992, aged just twenty six.

'Ah yes, Hillary I am certain about. She has been a sanguisuge for twenty four years and was turned by a particularly vicious tribe of predatory creatures. You must detect a pattern with all these details, surely? To turn a former hunter or slayer into the very creature that they hunt is so ironic. Rarely are hunters killed outright as it provides so much more of a satisfying conclusion to change them into the abominable beasts they so loathe and fear. But remember, whatever their current form, they will retain their mortal memories, even though they may have a very different physiognomy.'

'But they could be human-based and so not that different, couldn't they?'

'They could, it depends on the nature of the creature that did the turning.'

Erin felt a wave of unease wash through the family at the possible fate of their loved ones. Despite Dania's more enlightened frame of reference she thought that Dania was finding the feeling of disquiet oddly satisfying. So Dania did retain some animalistic tendencies. She looked around at the adult family focussing on reminiscences of their missing members, and the news of them that Dania had imparted. But as she did so, Erin realised that her decision to vote for an end to their hunter tradition was wavering. She felt an inner turmoil as conflicting emotions battled for supremacy.

'Your child is struggling with her conscience.'

The whole family looked at Dania before turning their gaze onto Erin. Erin gave a watery smile and looked around at the expectant faces before her.

'I didn't know about D'Arcy, Angela and Maud. Why has no one told me about these family members? Do we feel humiliated by them because we feel failure?'

Erin paused for a moment. 'I think I'm beginning to change my mind.'

She looked at Dania, who remained impassive, her milky white skin like polished marble.

'As we are still in the discussion phase child, nothing has been written in stone. It is down to you.'

Josephine's tone was sympathetic.

Erin frowned.

'It surely can't be right to leave family members to their unchosen fate. After all, they had no say in what happened to them. Joshua did not hesitate, did he?'

'But what we must remember is that all three of the most recent disappearances were venators who were actively hunting when they went missing. They were all aware of the dangers of what we do. But, that said, I am uncomfortable in leaving them to their fate. Maud was in the wrong place at the wrong time, while D'Arcy and Angela, forgive me, took the dangers too lightly,' said George.

Harold snorted derisively.

'So what's the alternative, George? Ask them whether they want to remain a sanguisuge or accept that one of us will put them out of their undead misery? We all know that it doesn't work like that! Once you become a sanguisuge you want to preserve your life, such as it is. Any thoughts of the creature they have become and the damage and havoc they could wreak are disregarded. All they want is to continue their existence whatever the cost, to themselves and others,' said Harold, his tone becoming harsher.

Silence prevailed. They all knew the truth in Harold's words.

'If I may?'

They all looked at Dania.

'I can provide a more enlightened perspective on what it means to be a sanguisuge.'

'I am sorry, please accept our apologies, it should be obvious to us all that you would have a more informed knowledge in these matters,' said Josephine.

'Thank yo...'

Dania stopped, frozen. Once again the mortals moved as one towards their concealed weapons. This time, Erin brought out a crucifix sensing, almost as a reflex, that danger was at hand. She turned to look at Dania, who shook her head slowly. Erin kept hold of it.

'Outside,' whispered Harold. He had moved nearer to the window and now he carefully lifted the curtain to one side and peered out into the darkness. A large flapping shadow of a beast met his eyes, staring straight back at him.

'I mean you no harm mortal. I bring a message from your relative...the one formerly known as Hillary Rossiter.'

The light from the bedroom illuminated the creature as Harold drew back the curtains more fully and opened the window a little further. He watched as the creature flared its flanged nostrils and tasted the air with its tripartite tongue.

'I can taste the blood flowing in your veins. Can you not feel desire welling within you, sanguisuge?'

Dania and Erin moved to the window and looked out. Dania called to the creature.

'I do not identify with you. I have renounced the sanguisuge calling with a blood oath.'

'How very noble of you. Aren't one of you mortals going to invite me in?'

Harold, as the senior active sanguisuge hunter in the family, moved towards the window once more.

'You can deliver your message from where you are.'

The creature attempted a smile but it merely transformed its visage into a hideous aspect, revealing its jaws laden with thin, sharp penetrating needles for teeth. This predator did not penetrate the jugular vein with two sharp fangs and leave two small puncture wounds, it ripped out the prey's throat.

'As you wish.'

The creature seemed to hover effortlessly, like a massive kestrel, barely expending much energy. The other family members went to the other bedroom window, although they did not open it more fully. They did not know what they were dealing with, after all.

'The mortal known as Hillary has accepted her life as a sanguisuge...completely. She has incorporated into the lineage and way of life and requires no rescuing, no release from her sanguisuge future in any form. Any attempt to do so would be met with hostility.'

'Can I ask a question?'

Listening to them, Erin could feel her decision beginning to consolidate. She felt different, more confident, as though she knew things that weren't common knowledge.

'That is why I am present at the time of this passing.'

The creature appeared to look beyond the window into the room itself and to the corpse of the former hunter. A strange expression passed across its face.

Erin addressed the creature, the family allowing her her head.

'Does the creature drink human blood?'

'It does.'

'Freely, without coercion?'

'We are based on a traditional culture. Mortals are prey, we are the predators, as it has always been. However, we do not slaughter indiscriminately. We only take what we need to survive.'

Erin grimaced.

'I see. Then maybe we shall meet again one day.'

The creature broke its features into an attempted laugh but all that escaped were guttural barks.

'You would rue the day, mortal. In any case are you not on the brink of terminating your atrocities against my kind?'

Erin glanced at Harold, both studying the creature before them.

'Are you not the juvenile who has ended history?'

Erin smiled.

'You are mistaken. I have taken no such decision.'

She felt the adult Stable family member's eyes upon her. They could all see and she could sense the change in her poise and posture, and her natural authority, elicited by the manifestation of the sanguisuge creature. She knew what they did not know. The creature spoke.

'I am in error then. What has wrought this change?'

Erin smiled knowingly.

'Your appearance before us...Aunt Hillary.'

There were gasps of incredulity. Only Dania appeared unfazed. The creature uttered a series of rasping barks again in mirth before flapping its wings and advancing towards the window.

'I am afraid it is you who is mistaken.'

As the creature moved closer to the window Erin watched as Harold intuitively moved his hand, which held the stake, into a more threatening position. She then looked at the beast which somehow gave the impression of being larger than it actually was. That said, she thought, it would present a formidable adversary.

'I don't think so.'

Erin's tone was sure, unwavering.

She didn't know how she knew that it was Hillary who floated before them. She could sense that Uncle Harold in particular could find no signs that the being before him had once been his sister. How had she come to that conclusion? She only knew that she was completely sure of herself, as though she had some skill, some talent, some sense that he and the others did not.

As Erin uttered the mortal identity of the creature before them, every member of the Stable family moved closer to see if they could detect anything that might indicate that she was correct. Hillary's brother George joined Harold and Erin. Hillary's parents, Robyn and Berkley remained at a distance, although they wouldn't have been able to explain why. Maybe doubt was preferable to certainty?

'I have fulfilled my obligation, mortals, and delivered the message I was charged with. How you respond I leave to you.'

The being made as if to turn and leave but then thought better of it.

'The House of Javier has its own monsters, does it not?'

Dania emerged from the family group.

'There are a number who remain limited and shackled by their lusts.'

'Limited? It may be that you find it advantageous in some future nightmare to resurrect some of your more base tendencies. There is unease and a sense of fear permeating through some of our kind, which should act as a warning to you all.'

'Then we shall be ready to face them, if and when that time comes,' said Erin.

'The little warrior has grown in stature. She has spirit for one so slight, and limited historical knowledge of how dark the night can become,' said the beast.

'I fear nothing with my family by my side and a light to expunge the darkness Aunt Hillary. Thank you for the warning.'

The creature contorted its face as though about to strike.

'You would do well little one, to heed the fate of a family member of similar age who once thought as you did. She no longer seeks the light.'

'You speak of Louella. What more do you know? I beg you to tell us,' Constance was fraught with agony as George's arm encircled her waist to support her.

'It is always an irony when those who hunt and despise us become one with us.'

The being paused, gazing upon the family.

'Only more so when they have been seduced and turned by one of their own.'

It took a moment or two for the depth and breadth of her words to sink in.

'Hillary turned Louella?'

Robyn's voice crackled.

The creature wriggled with pleasure at the affect of its testimony.

'No. Not Hillary.' She almost spat it out with distaste.

A dawning realisation swept through the family.

'Oh my god, not Davis...'

Robyn gasped at the memory of her lost brother and his passionate and wild ways.

'No...no ...'

Berkley moved closer to his wife who buried her face in his shoulders.

The creature looked directly at Erin before casting her gaze across the entire family. Her reptilian eyes came to rest on Dania.

'There are hostile forces ranged against you and your ilk that bode ill. You cannot possibly imagine the straits that will befall you.'

With that she was gone.

Erin looked around the group of adults before her. She knew that her next statement would seal all their fates.

'I vote to continue our traditions and uphold our protection of humanity. That WAS Hillary and it is our duty to confront all former family members, who, through no fault of their own, are no longer of mortal substance.'

She felt them all looking on her with affection and pride. Whatever their thoughts about the family heritage, they knew that it was safe in Erin's hands. Clearly she possessed some insights, some abilities similar to those that Joshua had shown throughout his life. She was his Great-Grandaughter.

She felt calm, confident about what she had decided. Another lesson learnt. It was never too late to change your mind.

Erin had come of age.

The End

Follow the Stable family in A Body Parts Cadaver Two and the whole collection of short stories in The Heart at Stake Archives – Coming Soon.

Printed in Great Britain
by Amazon